Making

Waves

VIVIENNE SAVAGE

Chapter 1

~ALESSA~

A cool morning breeze blew through the open windows, filling my beachside home with the ocean-scented wind. I breathed it in and finished sipping the steaming, green-tinted water in my ceramic tea mug. Once I'd had enough of the jasmine and green tea blend, I tipped the remaining liquid into the sink and breezed into the bathroom to start my day.

Part of my employment on the island included a small, private home away from the tourists. In less than a fifteen-minute walk I reached the beach, my swimsuit worn beneath jogging shorts. Most of the visitors didn't venture into the water until afternoon, choosing to fill their morning hours with the resort's attractions.

A lone figure ran along the damp sand where the water washed up over the shore. I recognized Kekoa immediately. Every morning like clockwork he jogged the same strip of land before heading into work as the owner's right hand man. He veered off his route and headed my way.

My eyes crept over him, losing the battle to maintain eye contact. Kekoa was an absolute hard-bodied fox with impressive muscles beneath smooth, golden-brown skin. Black tribal tattoos spread over his left shoulder and down his bicep, an intricate homage to his Pacific Islander ancestry.

I drooled over him often.

"Good morning, Kekoa."

"The same to you, Alessa. I'm glad I caught you, actually. Teo would like to see you during lunch."

I wonder what he wants. "Thanks. I'll be there." I waved and he continued his jog down the sandy curve.

The owner of the resort was tall, dark, handsome, and green-eyed, but with a name like Teotihuacan Arcillanegro, most of us called him by Teo for short. He's a nice guy, *if* you could call him a guy at all.

He's actually a dragon. I first found out the secret about him a couple years ago while freediving around one of his islands for a research project. Now I'm under an ironclad nondisclosure agreement that'll probably take me for everything I'm worth if I tell. So to avoid losing his friendship and paying out a devastating lawsuit, I kept my mouth shut, because silence was better than getting covered in whatever condiment a dragon prefers to dollop on his meals.

I don't think he'd really eat me, but some of us longtimers like to make macabre jokes. He even seemed like a different man since his wedding. Still intimidating, but also more approachable.

With Teo's request in mind, I checked into work for the day but kept an eye on the clock. The smell of saline water and marine animals surrounded me, a welcoming scent I'd come to love in the five years since my arrival on the island.

"Mornin', Alessa!" Julia called.

"Hey, girl."

"Cutting it a little close, aren't you?" My brunette friend grinned at me and pointed to the time. I was due to arrive fifteen minutes ago to begin my water sampling.

I sulked at her. "I'm the assistant manager. You're not supposed to call me out for being late."

"If I don't bust your proverbial balls, your head may get as big as the doctor's ego," she chirped happily.

"Ugh. Yeah. Bust away," I said with a grimace on my face.

Despite Isla de los Sueños' location off the Yucatán Peninsula, the resort's employees came from a wide background. On his private island, Teo made his own rules, hiring the people best for the job whether they were local or traveling from as far as Japan. Contrasting the laid-back dragon, our manager was a stiff-upper-lip kind of Brit with a dry, grating accent and a superiority complex.

I loved the resort. Unlike other parks with aquatic divisions, we didn't maintain captive animals. As an earth dragon, Teo had a unique gift, allowing him to communicate wants and needs to other creatures.

Every single animal was here because it wanted to be here, usually joining our crew for as little as a few days to as long as a couple of weeks. We had some repeat performers who enjoyed the attention from humans, so sometimes the same dolphin appeared three or four times in a year.

As an employee in the resort, I'd learned more about animals, their relationships, and how they viewed humans than I ever did while studying in college to become a marine biologist.

"Earth to Alessa. You better get on those samples before Doctor Castlebury arrives."

I snapped out of my daydream of swimming with the dolphins and hurried to collect my testing supplies. "Sorry. Long, sleepless night. I had all kinds of weird dreams about swimming in the ocean."

"It wasn't that shark dream again, was it?"

I shook my head and stepped over to one of the fish hatchery tanks. Teo was against the use of wild caught specimens in the aquariums, so we had established a captive bred marine fish program on the island. "No. This was different. I think I was swimming with someone."

"Someone sexy?" Julia ventured.

"Yeah. Maybe. It's hard to remember the details," I said.

As we fell into our usual routines, I caught up on my work then peeked in on the seahorse nursery. One of the dads was ready to pop, and at any moment, a swarm of little babies would spill from the delicate creature. I loved watching seahorse birth.

"So… normally I wouldn't bring this up, but he looked so pitiful I promised to at least ask. Ricardo is really sorry about how things went and wishes you'd unblock his number."

"Screw him. Your brother is a prick."

Julia sighed. "I'll pass it on."

We worked diligently until lunch when the alarm on my phone reminded me of Teo's request.

"I better go. The *big* boss wants to see me for lunch."

"Uh oh."

Judy, his secretary, greeted me with a big smile and a hug when I entered the administrative compound. "He's waiting for you in his office."

"Great." I stepped through the door and into tropical paradise. A few years back, his office was a barren square with a window and computer desk. Between Teo and his wife, it now rivaled one of the rainforest greenhouses littering the island.

A scarlet macaw perched beside the window. My entrance motivated it to shuffle and dance the length of the wooden pole beneath its gray feet. I laughed.

"Hi, Bailador," I greeted him. "I love you, too."

"And where is my hello?" Teo demanded.

My sexy-as-sin boss rose to his feet. Instead of business suits and extravagant office clothing, he and Kekoa wore beach attire and board shorts during their days in the office. With his shirt worn open, it revealed the golden strip of skin between his pecs and his perfect six pack.

"I guess you get a hello, too. Hi, Teo. Kekoa said you wanted to see me, what's up?"

"First, have some sushi," he replied, passing a neat package to me. The scent of hot mayo and wasabi emanated from within.

"Why are you buttering me up before I even have a chance to sit down?"

"Harper flew home to Australia last night. Her mother's ill again."

One hand raised to my mouth. "Oh no," I whispered.

"She may not pull through this time, so I've given Harper time off until her mother goes into remission or..."

Teo is a good man. Dragon. Dragon-man, I thought.

"So I'd like you to replace her in the mermaid program until the end of the season."

"*What?*"

"There's no one else on the island qualified to do it."

"Teo, I swim with a tank or an air line these days—"

"Kekoa mentioned you were freediving again last week. He swam past you."

Damn. I searched for another excuse to bow out of shimmying into a too-tight silicone mermaid tail and a revealing bikini top.

"It was very impressive," Kekoa agreed from the door as he entered. Coming from a wereshark, it was the best compliment anyone could receive. "You were underwater for nearly six minutes before you surfaced."

And he timed me? What the hell.

"Will you do this for me, Alessa? No one has come close to replacing you since you promoted into the aquatics division."

Without giving a prompt answer, I cracked open the lid of the sushi to-go box and fished out a piece. After savoring the tangy bite of eel sauce, I squinted across the desk to my boss. I sighed. "Maybe you should slide on a tail and dive into the tank," I teased him. "I don't know, Teo. It's been a couple years and I've gained weight. Plus Castlebury will have a fit if he finds out you took me away. You know this is the time of year when he's out there hunting for his mystery sea beast."

Teo rolled his eyes. "*I* will deal with Doctor Castlebury," he assured me. "This will be until

Harper returns, and I have budgeted twice the usual salary…"

My eyes lit up. Double pay would be enough to finish paying off my college tuition loans. "Deal. I'll try my old tail on when I get home."

That wasn't good enough for Teo, who informed me Kekoa had arrived to take my measurements. Anticipating my agreement, he'd already contacted an artist to create my new tail. After he called me behind the desk to take a seat beside him, we scrolled through dozens of design possibilities on the woman's site.

When asked about the cost of paying me double the wages to flaunt my swim skills, on top of the cost to build me a new suit, Teo laughed.

"It's not about the money. It's the experience. My guests come to this resort expecting to see amazing things. The return of investment comes when your photos wind up on social media, providing free advertisement—"

"If you really want to expand the attraction, you'll have Kekoa or one of the other hot guys squeezing into a tail. The ladies want mermen. We want rippling abs and Adonis belts on display while hot guys perform their best Michael Phelps impressions."

Teo rubbed his chin, his eyes lighting up with interest.

Bingo. The girls were going to owe me for this one.

"Teo, do not listen to her. No one wants to see me in a merman tail," Kekoa disagreed.

"Rippling abs, Teo. Think of how Marcy loves to touch yours. Think of the ROI as needy women hemorrhage money to see his pecs."

I stole a glance at Kekoa to find him glowering at me.

"I win," I mouthed to him.

No one could change a dragon's mind once money was involved.

Chapter 2

~DANTE~

Five months. I had five months to soak in life among the humans and spend time with the man who raised me.

Warm sand shifted between my bare toes as I made my way across the beach, eager for the breath of fresh air brought by civilization.

It would take days before I acclimated to the sun, no longer used to its heat against my skin. It tightened my flesh, reddening my ears within moments of leaving Abuelo's home. A thousand smells assaulted my nose, reminding me of the contrast between human settlements and the vast ocean. As I passed a vendor peddling sweet treats, cinnamon and sugar wafted to me on the wind. My mouth watered, but I resisted and moved on to the path.

Once I reached the administrative compound, Teo's secretary smiled and gestured for me to take a seat.

"He'll be right with you, Dante. Are you back to join us for another season?"

"I am."

"How was your journey?"

Quiet. Lonely. The usual. With a phony smile on my face, I told her the news she wanted to hear, "Great."

"I'm so glad to hear it. The beach just isn't the same without you. Maybe we can pick up those lessons…"

"Dante! You're back!" Alessa collided against me, warm skin and fresh-smelling cotton. The wild fragrance of plumeria clung to her hair as warm lips touched my cheek. "When did you come back to town?"

"Last night," I answered with a chuckle. I squeezed her in return, lifting her from the floor. She was shorter than me by over half a foot, typical female height to my above average frame.

"And you didn't come to say hi to me? I'm insulted." She sniffed daintily, putting on a wounded expression for show.

"You know how Abuelo is once I return to the island."

"True. He's been lonely without you." Alessa bit her lower lip, appearing as if she had more to say.

"You look great. How have you been?"

Alessa swatted at my arm. "You'd know if you, you know, wrote or called once in a while."

"I told you. There's no internet where my family lives, and I can't walk to a library on a whim to use a computer."

I returned one year to discover Abuelo had told all of my new human friends I lived in a piss-poor Sicilian village without internet or technology. He claimed I'd saved all year to visit against my father's wishes.

That my dad thought the city life would ruin me.

Abuelo couldn't be closer to the truth.

While it did hurt to fib to Alessa, everything said to her was technically true.

"What are you doing here in the office?" I asked for a change of topic. "I thought you'd be fussing over Kai or one of your other projects as usual," I said, referring to the resort's resident green sea turtle. I'd been the one who found the injured creature two summers ago and Alessa was one of his main caregivers.

"Teo asked to see me during lunch, and I was just leaving. He even plied me with gifts to bribe me." She held up a large to-go container full of sushi.

"Getting into trouble already?"

"Hardly." She laughed. "Harper had a family emergency come up so she flew back to Sydney. Teo asked if I'd take her spot for the rest of summer in the mermaid program."

"Can you even swim in one of those things? Those phony fins are huge."

She swatted my shoulder, barely budging me. "I was one of Teo's first mermaids, you ass. I'm like a fish once I have my fins on, thank you very much."

Kekoa peeked his head out of the office. "He is ready for you now."

"Better not keep him waiting. We'll catch up later once I'm off the clock," Alessa said. She headed out with her food so I walked into the office. Kekoa shut the door behind me.

"Ah, Dante. You've been missed, my friend." Teo rose from the chair and met me halfway across the floor. The dragon always carried the aroma of soil and green leaves on his skin. As an earth dragon, wild plant life was part of his nature.

After a solid embrace, he urged me to take a seat with him on the office balcony. "Coffee?"

"Hell yeah."

Kekoa poured mugs for all of us and then he settled in the chair beside me. "If we knew to expect you, we would have had more of your favorite things waiting for you. Maybe some time you will remember to inform us that you have returned."

I pointedly ignored his comments. Alessa was always on my case about my tendency to arrive and leave without warning. One nag was enough. "Thanks." I blew across the surface of the heavily-caffeinated brew. Cocoa, chili, and cinnamon was carried to me on the steam, the coffee flavored with rich Mexican chocolate.

"I missed this," I groaned happily. It was too hot, scalding my mouth, but I didn't care and sipped from it again.

Teo grinned. "I will make sure your grandfather has a fresh supply."

"Appreciated. So, am I allowed to resume my old job again now that I'm here?" I was eager to hit the surf and to share my knowledge of the waves. As a seasonal resort employee, I enjoyed the best of both worlds — life among civilization and fun in the ocean.

"Of course. I give you the same answer every year. It's tourist season, and many want surfing lessons. Kekoa eased the burden on some of the instructors by assisting in your absence, but it is not his preferred use of time."

The wereshark nodded, a sour expression on his face.

"What's not to prefer about it? Do you dislike the college coeds fawning over you in their bikinis?" I asked. That was exactly the problem.

"Meh," he grumbled. "Empty-headed. I have no desire to spend my time with a woman who lacks substance."

"All of them aren't that bad."

He shot me a dirty look. "So *you* say."

We laughed and caught up, indulging in friendly banter and chat about Teo's life with a mortal woman. Whenever I returned, I found him changed for the better, an improvement over the sour dragon who once haunted the island.

I envied him.

With each passing year, females among my kind became fewer and fewer. Males battled one another for the privilege of courting our women and winning didn't always mean we'd earn their affection. Last year was my final chance to find a mate.

I was out of time, assigned to the rear guard as underwater infantry for the herd. Despite the dismal outlook toward my future, I looked forward to my last visit on dry land. The rear guard was a death sentence in a way, our equivalent of serving in the armed forces. Unlike the boys in uniform, we didn't receive guns, leave time, or salary. Most of the new recruits didn't last more than two or three years before becoming a meal for an orca or great white.

"Give Roberto my best," Teo said as I rose from my seat. "We've missed his stall at the weekend festival."

"And his food. No one fries fish as well as Roberto," Kekoa remarked. "He hasn't opened up on the beach at all."

I raised a brow. "What? How long has this been going on?"

"Almost a month. When I called over the weekend to inquire about his health, he said he'd return soon and not to worry," Teo said.

"I'll get to the bottom of it."

When I arrived home, I didn't find my grandfather waiting on the porch with a cigar, or in his work shed creating another beautiful sculpture for the kiln.

"Abuelo?" I called, walking into the house.

A soft hum emanated from the rear room. It ended abruptly when I shut the door behind me. I pushed forward and moved into the single bedroom of his small bungalow where I caught him shutting the closet door. His cheeks were pale, his breaths labored and uneven.

"Abuelo?"

"Don't you know how to knock anymore?" He pressed his blue lips together in a disapproving, thin line. "Or did you forget while you were at sea?"

"Your door was open," I pointed out. "But you're hiding something from me. Why?"

Nothing prepared me for his answer. With resignation on his weathered face, he came out with the truth.

"I'm sick, Dante."

"Sick with what? Cold?"

He wasn't coughing or runny-nosed, but his strange breathing pattern troubled me. Like he couldn't pull the air into his lungs.

"No. I wish it were so simple. A bad illness nearly killed me over the winter while you were gone. I spent two weeks in the hospital and even longer here in bed to recuperate."

His words chilled my blood, numbing my fingertips and toes. Abuelo had always been there for me and more of a father than the stallion who conceived me. The thought of him alone, suffering in his sick bed without help, twisted my stomach.

Unless… "Who took you to the hospital?"

"Alessa did." He coughed a few times into his elbow then gestured to the closet. "I need my machine. I didn't want you to know about it, but the cat's out of the bag now."

"Why not? Why keep it from me, Abuelo?"

"I don't want you to worry about me while you're away over the winter months. I have an illness, and it's not going to get better."

"Is it the flu?" I asked, clueless. We didn't catch it, but I'd seen lots of humans suffering from it.

My grandfather shook his head. "It's called chronic obstructive pulmonary disease." I stared at him. His words were Greek to me, just a string of medical jargon that made no sense. "It means my lungs don't work the way they used to," he clarified.

"Is it deadly?"

"It can be."

I dragged the machine out again. He had a small canister of oxygen and tubing with two small prongs. Within moments of positioning it into place, the color returned to his lips and the difficult breathing eased.

I sat beside my old man on the bed and he laid one weary arm around my shoulders. We talked, he told me about the difficult winter, and I struggled to come to terms with the meaning of his words.

My grandfather, the man who saved my life and taught me to be a human, would die in the next couple of years.

And I wouldn't be present to hold his hand and watch him go.

***

Alessa would never forgive me if I didn't pop in for a spontaneous visit. Once I'd had some time to adjust to the idea of losing Abuelo, I helped him mix a fresh batch of batter for his stand.

Then he kicked me the hell out of his place. "Go see your girl."

"She isn't my girl."

Abuelo chuckled and told me off in Spanish. I vamoosed and made my way to the aquatics center to capitalize on all the free time I had until my usual clients began booking surf lessons.

"Hey, Dante!" Pam called. The blonde girl shot me a grin and a big wave with her free hand. She worked with a pair of tongs over a marine environment filled with colorful sea urchins and coral. I salivated. They saw beautiful creatures; I saw dessert.

"Hola, señorita. Where's Alessa?"

"Arguing with the boss. I'm waiting to talk to her too, so grab a number."

Grumbling, I pushed my way toward Alessa's office anyway but stopped short when I heard the raised voices. *Shit.*

"Look, he's your boss, too. He asked me to do this as a personal favor to him," Alessa argued.

"Of course. Any reason to shirk your responsibilities. Had I known you would become so unreliable, I would have promoted Julia in your place." The snide scientist's voice made my skin crawl.

Doctor Castlebury might have been a top notch marine biologist, but he was also a first class asshole. His snooty accent made it sound like he was always talking down to you.

"That isn't true and you know it. Teo sank a lot of—"

"Teo?" The doctor laughed. "Are we on a first name basis now with the owner of the resort?"

"Everyone calls him by his name," Alessa snapped back. "I can still help with the morning test samples and we do any cleaning at night anyway when the guests aren't around."

"And how shall we care for these animals? Your injured sea turtle?"

Guilt gnawed at my belly, a consequence of my shameless eavesdropping, but the entire conflict was like a train wreck; once I heard it, I couldn't move away.

"Kai is doing fine. He chooses to stay in the cove and he doesn't need much."

"He should be set loose in the wild where he belongs," Castlebury chastised.

"We tried that and he swam back. This island's reefs are his home now."

I stepped away from the door, suppressing the urge to burst through it and trample her boss into the ground. I could have made him a greasy smear on the carpet, but respect for Teo's rules kept my wild beast at bay.

Unable to listen to him heap abuse on her, I sat facing one of the tanks. A graceful yellow tang glided through the water, occasionally pausing to graze on a piece of seaweed wafer. I smiled.

Yellow tangs were one of my favorites, too visually stunning to consider food.

"Just try firing me," Alessa seethed from the opening door, her hand on the knob. "You can't."

"Go play at being a fish tart if that's what you truly want," came the dismissive reply from within the room. "Who am I to stop you?"

Asshole, I thought.

Alessa nearly blew past me, her irritated gaze focused on the floor. I reached out and caught her by the hand then tugged her back and into my lap. She toppled into me with a soft "oof" of surprise.

"Look at the tang. She's being flashy today." A pair of clownfish darted out and circled the sunny yellow fish.

"Buttercup comes out a lot lately." Her hand lowered to my shoulder from its mid-slap position. "Jeez, you scared me. Where'd you come from?"

"My mother."

"Ha. Ha. Cute."

I beamed at her. "Cuter than Abuelo?"

"Eh." Alessa lifted her hand and turned it back and forth in a so-so gesture. "Close call. Really though, what are you doing in here?"

"Looking for you."

"Well, you found me. What's up?"

"Come out with me tonight," I said. After putting up with Castlebury's bullshit, she deserved an evening of carefree drinking and dance.

"I don't know…" She bit her lower lip. "I have to be here early tomorrow to catch up on inventory stuff before my days in the mermaid tank begin."

"C'mon, there's a band playing tonight and drink specials at the beach bar. You'll have a good time," I insisted.

Alessa's expression was torn, so I cheated and danced my fingers across her ticklish ribs. She wriggled in my lap and laughed, squirming to get free, but I didn't let up.

"Say you'll come out with me and I'll stop."

Her giggles and squeals echoed across the room. The yellow tang and her clownfish pals darted back inside the colorful coral growths.

"Okay!" Alessa cried out, breathless from laughter. "I'll go. I'll go!"

"Good. Come on."

"But I'm working!"

"Pam, can you cover whatever crap she has to do?"

Pam offered a silent salute with her metal tongs. Grinning, I pulled Alessa through the aquatics complex. The hexagonal building had grown in the months since my last appearance. I hurried past the brand new shark exhibit without looking, a shiver running down my spine inspired by memories of encountering the monstrous beasts while in the ocean. Hippocampi were their prey, but thanks to Kekoa we were safe in these waters.

"Hey." I sucked in a breath. "Thanks for looking out for my grandfather. I appreciate it." We moved across the paved walkway without a destination in mind.

"He told you, huh?"

I nodded. "He said you popped in almost every day to check on him this winter, and you were the one to make him go to the hospital on the mainland. I wouldn't have him anymore if not for you. Thanks."

"You don't have to thank me for it, Dante. It's what anyone would have done."

How long had it been since I first returned to land, searching for the man who saved my life? Thirteen years ago, I could barely speak a lick of English. With the help of Abuelo and Teo, I'd learned enough to get by. I picked up the rest while instructing my clients.

"He's all you have now, right?"

I shook my head. "My dad is still alive, but he doesn't approve of me coming out this way, you know? He doesn't think of Abuelo as family, but I do. If not for him finding me on the beach, Teo could have never gotten me back to my family."

Alessa nodded in sympathy and rubbed my shoulder. "His sickness isn't a death sentence, Dante. We still have years left with him."

You may, but I won't.

***

"When did you start dancing like a male stripper?" Alessa demanded. "What the hell, Dante?"

"What? What's wrong with the way I dance?"

"There's nothing wrong with it, you know, if a guy is wearing a banana hammock for me to stuff dollar bills inside," she said, flustered.

"It's the same as I've always danced." At least I didn't feel like I was doing anything different.

"Ha. If you say so. Who are you showing off for?" She made a show of scoping out our surroundings, likely scouting for a client of mine. I wasn't fazed by the rumors anymore.

The combined effect of the heat, our mixed drinks, and dancing brought a rosy flush to her cheeks and the glow of sweat to her skin. She smelled divine. In close quarters, I couldn't ignore the floral scent drifting to me, mingled with Alessa's natural smell.

What is that smell always surrounding her? I wondered. Beneath the floral perfume of shampoo and body splash, I frequently caught a whiff of the ocean. Salt water. Like it was part of Alessa's soul.

"Alessa!"

The tenor voice calling out her name took the wind out of my sails. Alessa's smile faded, replaced by the scowl I'd worked so hard to wipe away.

"Save it, Ricardo. I already told you, I'm done talking."

"That's it? I mess up one time and you're done with me? I thought I meant something to you."

"For Chrissake, take the break-up like a man." Alessa raised a hand for another drink. The bartender placed a shot glass full of tequila down beside a plate with lemon wedges and salt.

Ricardo's expression contorted into a mask of hate. I winced and looked away, focusing on my cerveza.

"You got someone else then?" He paused, as if to consider his accusation, and before Alessa could deny it he continued. "Like anyone would want your fat ass, *puta* bitch. Go spread your legs for someone el—"

I jumped out of my seat and between them, placing myself in his face. "I think you need to go before all the liquor you've drank makes a bigger fool of you, Ricardo." The strong scent of tequila reached me, worsened by my close proximity to him. My nostrils flared as I breathed it in, my attention fixed on his bloodshot eyes. Her ex-boyfriend was a sip away from a case of alcohol poisoning.

"You got a problem, Dante? This is between me and Alessa. You go and mind your own business."

Despite her ex's bodybuilder bulk, the macho act didn't intimidate me; I towered above Ricardo by a good five inches and had natural, athletic muscle. For Alessa, I'd snap him in half with my bare hands. "You involved me in this when you disrespected her in front of me."

Ricardo stood his ground. So did I. From the corner of my eye, I saw the bartender moving closer to the phone and a member of resort security weaving toward us through the dance crowd.

"Fine. You keep her then." Ricardo made a parting comment I couldn't translate, but from the heat rising to Alessa's face, I knew it had to be bad. Once he was gone, I turned to face my friend and found her facing the bar with her head down on her folded arms.

"Hey? Lessa? I didn't mean to embarrass you." I set my hand between her shoulder blades. She was warm beneath my hand, her smooth back covered in a fine layer of dewy sweat.

"I think I'm done for the night."

"Wanna walk it off?"

She shrugged without lifting her head. "May as well exercise my fat ass off."

Unbridled anger washed over me. *There's nothing wrong with her ass.*

"Come on. The coast by your place should be quiet right now."

"Whatever." Alessa slid off her stool and headed out, but at a slow pace with her arms wrapped tight around herself. I managed to convince her to step out of her strappy heels. Together, we walked barefoot over the damp sand where the foamy surf came in with the tide. It was warm beneath my feet, heat lingering despite the loss of the sun.

I seethed along the way. Every time I opened my mouth to speak, the words on the tip of my tongue felt too trite for consoling her. "Your ass isn't fat," I finally said as her place came into view.

"You're just saying that," she moped.

"Why would I lie to you? I have nothing to gain from making up things. Ricardo is a dick."

"Yeah, I'll agree with you there. I don't even know what I saw in him. Guess that's why it was such a short fling." She sighed and let her shoulders droop more.

"Want me to beat him up? Bury him in the sand? I can do that, you know. There's enough of him to feed a thousand sea creatures."

A small smile tugged her lips. "He'd make the beach smelly." She stumbled on the sand, a misstep of her foot.

"Damn. True." I slyly snuck my arm around Alessa's shoulders to steady her. The same alluring scent tickled my senses again. "Whatever you're wearing smells nice, by the way."

"Huh?" She blinked. "Oh. Thanks. I put flowers in my bath sometimes when I wanna soak."

Dreading the sight of her house in the distance, I tried to stall with small talk. Anger at Ricardo made me desperate to put the smile firmly on her face again before we parted ways. "Remind me to call you next time I want to smell pretty. Do I get to come in and eat you out of house and home since we missed out on our chance for dinner?"

"I dunno. Last time I let you in my fridge you complained about my lack of veggies."

"You won't hear a complaint from me this time. I will eat Pop-Tarts and grin through *every* bite."

I did. By the time she nodded off to sleep, I was on a strawberry-filling induced sugar high. But my friend had a smile on her face well worth the price of my sleepless night.

Chapter 3

~DANTE~

The appointments came hard and fast over the next days, packed together on a tight schedule to appease the demand for my services. Repeat customers returned from last year, eager to advance to the next step in their training.

Alessa believed I spent more time dipping my cock into my students than sliding a board onto the surf. It wasn't true and hadn't been since my first year as an instructor, when I was fresh to the world, eager to please any woman on two legs, and blown away by how good sex could feel.

I didn't have the honor of breeding in the herd, so I quickly became addicted to receiving any form of attention on land. Abuelo even sat me down for the talk, plied me with condoms, and set me free again until frequent sex with an endless line of willing females began to bore me.

They still bored me. No-strings-attached sex was okay for a while until the beast in me wanted — needed — more.

I spent my hour lunch break drifting aimlessly until a moving crowd caught my eye. Teo's island had a strict event schedule, filling each day with activities and shows.

I never kept up with the schedule, and had no idea where they were going, but our destination became clear once the shuffling gait took us below ground.

A fair-skinned mermaid drifted past, golden hair streaming behind her. I hadn't watched one of the mermaid shows before, too disinterested in watching humans playing at a life they could never understand.

The real mermaids of the paranormal world were terrifying, man-eating beasts. They'd laugh at the humans wearing silicone tails and green bikini tops.

Alessa is in there somewhere, I thought, intrigued.

"Mommy, are the mermaids real?" the child beside me asked her mother. She couldn't have been more than three or four, with rosy-red cheeks and a head of blonde hair.

"Of course they are."

"I wanna be a mermaid."

An ethereal beauty glided by the aquarium glass, her fiery red hair adrift in the water. Her blue tail held hints of green and gold iridescence and the flowing fin faded into gold and ruby at the tips. Seaweed, pearls, and artistically placed fish netting made up her bikini top.

Wide grey eyes peered at me from the tank. Eyes I knew.

I hadn't been prepared for the effect she would have on me, blown away by my failure to recognize Alessa at a glance. My heart rate spiked and began to climb, the rapid pulse a methodic bass pounding in my ears.

She's gorgeous.

Alessa favored modest swimwear while on the beach and I'd never seen her in less than rash guard shirts and board shorts. As she floated on the current and twisted a somersault beneath the surface, I received a spectacular view of her body. An odd contrast of toned athleticism and generous curves made watching her a delight. She was soft in all of the right places, her breasts more than a handful, but tastefully concealed.

Desire hit me hard and fast, a sudden freight train sweeping away my common sense and ability to reason.

Alessa is my friend, I repeated while approaching the glass to stare at her. As I watched her perform for the crowd I couldn't take my eyes off her. She twisted and turned through the water, a beautiful sea nymph who enchanted the younger viewers and enraptured the adult males.

I didn't want them watching her. Hot jealousy washed through me followed by the urge to charge all the leering men in the room. My wild, animalistic instinct called for me to drive off the other male contenders. Only then, could I dive into the tank to claim my mate.

Whoa. The reckless path my thoughts took made me step back. *It's Alessa. This can't be right. She's a human.*

It happened rarely among my kind, known occurrences of fated mates happening so infrequently even *we* chalked it up as a fairy tale. Mating among the hippocampi was never about love; it was about violence and the stallion with the biggest hooves.

Alessa saw me through the glass and smiled. Her shoulders moved and tiny bubbles of air slipped from her. She'd giggled underwater, pleasing the small children in the audience and capturing my heart in one breath. Numb, I waved back to her.

"Mommy, it's Ariel!"

I'd never noticed it before, but the resemblance was uncanny.

"Hi," I mouthed to her.

She blew me a kiss and kicked to the surface for air.

I had to get out of here. I turned and weaved through the building crowd, desperate to reach the water. A swim was exactly what I needed.

They could reschedule the rest of my lessons.

***

I dove into the crystal-blue water and dolphin kicked to the sandy bottom. The natural embrace of the cool ocean became a comforting balm, easing my worries in an instant. Once my board shorts were weighed beneath a rock a few yards from the shore, I shifted to my natural state.

There was no greater freedom than shedding my human form, no matter the joy I felt in exploring their world above.

The world my mother once loved.

Over two decades had passed since her death, and over the course of that time, my memory of my mother had diminished. I could recall the color of her hair and little else, remembering only because we shared the same blue-black shade.

My tail whipped behind me, powerful muscle covered in glittering blue and purple scales. Dark horses like me were held in disdain, a bad omen among our kind who favored fair pelts and shining scales in pearlescent hues.

I cut through the water with efficient strokes, using my forelegs as flippers to maneuver through the reef. I swam for a half hour before the first hippocampi came into view, a small family of four: a mare, stallion, their young colt, and a newborn foal. The children grazed on ocean kelp while their mother nibbled a captured jellyfish.

Flicking my tail behind me, I glided forward and through a massive split in the rock formation, into the underground cavern we called home. When I broke surface, I climbed up and pulled my heavy bulk onto the rocks. The tropical paradise was crowded but safe, lit by thin shafts of sunlight spilling through fissures in the stone above. Here, we slept in rotations and fed from the greenery sprouting from the cavern walls.

An enormous stallion lay upon the bank beside his smaller mare. His pelt shone like liquid gold, his immense tail like mother of pearl. The fan at the tip of it resembled a starburst, vibrant as the morning sun. Adon, the massive stallion upon the rocks, did not move to acknowledge me. He barely raised his head, my presence too insignificant to be worthy of attention. It hurt and as usual I tried to ignore it.

"Father," I spoke up, channeling my thoughts through our link. I'd seen my father in his human shape twice in all of my life. Once, when he came on land to find me as a child. Again, a few years later when a troublesome group of sirens moved in on our territory back in Greece. The memory was murky at best.

"Be gone if you've come with meaningless news of your mortal world." His voice radiated through my mind, filled with the power and influence of an elder hippocampus. I shrank back instinctively.

I'm an adult now. He can't scare or hurt me anymore. Once I regained my conviction, I raised my head and leveled my eyes at him. "I do come with news," I said. "And a humble request for your advice."

The stallion raised his head and finally faced me, curiosity revealed in his formerly impassive features. I never asked for advice. "Speak."

"What do you know of fated mates, Father? Are they fable or truth?"

"They are a rare gift, but far from story. It is said the creature who finds his fated mate will enjoy a life twice blessed. But why do you ask? This is not advice, but a question."

"I ask because I may have met mine, Father. And she is as beautiful inside as she is to my eyes. I know there is a great chance she will feel for me as I do for her." Unless humans lacked the same instant attraction. The niggling thought snaked through my mind. I'd have to ask Teo's wife to be certain.

"Oh?" Adon watched me, intrigued. A hint of emotion almost showed in his equine face, but I knew better.

He hated me.

"What is this filly's name? I had believed all of breeding age to be mated and properly claimed."

"It's... She is not a filly, Fa—"

True happiness seeped into the strong mental voice. A chuckle of amusement followed. My dad hadn't laughed at anything I'd said to him since I was a colt. "Ahh, then a widowed mare. Not what I would have chosen for you, but respectable. Kind. Who is she, son?"

I ripped the figurative Band-Aid clean off, speaking in a rush. "Her name is Alessa, and she's human."

The pleasure faded, vanished like a popped bubble. He stared at me at first, a silent horse waiting for the punchline to a bad joke. "Absurd. There is no such thing as courtship and mating between a hippocampus and human," he snapped.

"I felt it, Father. I have never experienced anything of the like in all of my life. It was real."

"You desperately seek fulfillment in a world outside of our own. Had you shown as much interest in our kind as you do of the stinking apes above, perhaps you would have a mate, Dante."

I flinched. "I did everything possible, Father. Everything. I danced, I sang, I brought gifts and fought ocean predators for Calista to no avail. You and I both know it has nothing to do with my courtship efforts, and everything to do with my looks!"

Adon peered down his long muzzle at me and snorted.

"Is this why you hate me so much? Because I resemble Mother?"

He didn't answer me directly. The pearl-furred mare at his side had moved, relocating to the water and swimming away to a more peaceful location. We lacked a word for stepmother in our language, but I had only one mother and would not call Delia mine.

"Your mother's fascination with the humans caused her death. It will do the same to you. Your courtships fail because you give the topside more focus than your own kind."

"I don't—"

"Had you devoted this time to meeting and playing with our fillies this season, you may have met a match willing to accept a dark horse, and I would not be forced to relegate you to the guard. I have never felt more shame."

"But—"

"Remove yourself from my sight," he commanded.

My head drooped. "As you wish." Ending my audience with my father, I dove into the water and hurried away.

Maybe he was right. Maybe I had no one to blame but myself for my irrational attraction to the topside world. I swam as if Hades—or maybe even Poseidon himself—chased me from the ocean depths, tail churning the water behind me, forelegs aching and sore by the time I returned to the island.

Maybe, if I hadn't chased after a life on the surface, I'd have a true life down below.

Balmy, tropical air and an ocean breeze blew across my wet skin once I was on land again. I maintained full control of my emotions as I crossed the beach and retired to Abuelo's home.

The soft hum of the oxygen machine welcomed me, as did the man in his recliner. He waved from a seat in front of the television, enjoying a thick slice of flan brought to him by one of the neighbors.

"Want some?"

"No thanks."

A hot shower washed the salt and sand from my skin then I filled my belly with the fish tacos

Gramps had left over from the daily menu. I settled beside him, and together we watched some silly action flick he'd picked up at one of the resort shops.

"Abuelo, I have to tell you something."

"Oh?"

"Yes, but it's difficult to express."

Grandfather's expression softened. "You are going to the sea and not coming back."

"Yes." The ache in my heart didn't ease, making my words quiet and tight. *How did he know?*

"I had a feeling such a day would come. You've always been drawn to the ocean. And of course, it is where you belong."

Yeah… drawn to it, I thought. *Better to let him think I'm happy to go, than to worry for me every day.* "But what about you?"

"I got along just fine before you returned," he said. He laughed warmly and squeezed my arm. "I'll miss you, Dante, but you have to live your own life."

"But who will take care of you?"

"I told you not to worry about me. There are good folk on this island. Ever since my Catalina passed away, Teo and his people have been a family to me. Alessa too. We'll make do."

His words failed to loosen the knot in my chest. Abuelo had never given me anything but unconditional love and respect since finding me on the beach as a child. Leaving him felt as if I were abandoning my only true family.

But what choice do I have?

"Have you told Alessa yet?" he asked, pulling me from my inner thoughts.

"No. I wanted to talk to you first."

"Make sure you do. She's been a good friend to you, and to me. Don't wait 'til the day you leave."

"I… You're right. Dropping it on her and going would be wrong. Cruel."

"Smart boy."

Chapter 4

~ALESSA~

"This almost feels like a date," I teased. Humid air surrounded me as I breathed in the scent of green leaves and sweet orchids. Native island plant life grew wild, tamed only as needed for hikers and visitors on the trail. I held my sandals in one hand, delighting in cool soil beneath my feet.

"It's not."

"Are you sure? I expected you to bust out the sexy Italian at any moment."

Dante's warm laughter created butterflies in my belly. "I don't know that much of it," he said.

"So, how is it that you speak English so well but you don't know Italian? Even I can speak fluent Greek and I've only been there part of my life."

He laughed. "I've been coming here since I was a teen, remember? Abuelo is always complaining about me speaking English better than Spanish, too, but I can't help it when English is the primary language on the island. Most of the tourists come from America."

Dante and I walked side by side. He led me off the public trails into the private zone marked for cabana rentals. Small signs on wooden stakes led visitors where they belonged and told me we headed toward cabana #9.

He'd lured me out with promises of a swim race, so I'd dressed for it beneath my t-shirt and shorts by donning a green and purple bikini. It was the most revealing thing I'd ever purchased, but I wanted him to see my body without the giant silicone tail ruining the view.

"I lied to you," Dante finally admitted before the silence became awkward. "I'm not really from Italy."

"Huh?"

"I brought you out here to talk about something important. Something you should know. How much do you know about shapeshifters?"

"Silly, I know all about shapeshifters. I work for Teo, remember? I've known about him and Kekoa for a while now."

"I know, but there's… I never told you that I'm also one." His gaze held intensity I never saw before, studying my face and watching for my reaction. When I didn't move away or recoil in fear, he continued. "It's part of the reason why I'm only present until fall. My herd migrates."

"Herd? Then… you're not a wereshark like Kekoa or a dragon like Teo… what are you?"

My best friend wasn't human? He'd fooled me, but in hindsight a thousand warning signs swam to the surface.

He didn't have a driver's license. He could barely do more than basic math and had absolutely no knowledge of world events.

Dante offered me the opportunity to sit on one of the stone benches bordering the walking path, but I waved it off and continued walking alongside him.

"I'm a hippocampus."

"Like an enormous seahorse? Or… a… water horse? Neeeeigh," I said, waving a hand for emphasis.

"Like a water horse," Dante confirmed.

"I… I like horses," I said dumbly.

He grinned. "This was easier than I thought it would be."

"You brought me all the way out here to tell me that you're a paranormal creature? Dante, you could have told me while I was making us dinner." I leaned against him and bumped his hip with mine, his body heat familiar and inviting.

"I know, I know. It's…" He dragged in a breath. "I have more to say than that."

"More?"

We reached our designated cabana, a small hut with wooden support beams and heavy walls of straw and grass. A wicker basket awaited us with a bucket of chilled ice and a bottle of wine beside two coolers. I recognized Teo's handiwork, having helped him once to prepare something similar for his anniversary. He'd implemented my suggestions and improvements by providing futons for couples with kinky plans of open-door sex.

"What the hell? It's not my birthday, is it?" One of the small cooler boxes held an intricate edible bouquet. I plucked one of the flower shaped pieces of apple and a few grapes from the top.

"No," Dante said. "It's not."

"What's with the surprise and the wine?" I picked up another wooden skewer from the bouquet then peeked into the second cooler. Rows of my favorite sushi rolls greeted me. I breathed in the wasabi, pleased with Dante's considerate gift. "You're the best friend."

"No I'm not."

"You are, too. You did all of this for me?"

He nodded. "Yeah, I did. But there's something I need to tell you."

"Okay?"

He inhaled a deep breath, consternation wrinkling his brow. I noticed the circles beneath his eyes for the first time. That he was stressed. "I brought you here to break some bad news to you as gently as I could. It's my last summer visit. I won't be coming back to the island again."

At first, I waited for the rest of the joke. *He's joking. He has to be joking. Why would he go away forever like that?* Then I saw the pain in his eyes and knew that he was serious. "What? *Why?* What about your grandfather? You can't leave him.

He's sick! Did he tell you about how hard this winter was on him?"

"I told him a few days ago and he understands."

"But you can't… why?" I demanded, voice rising shrilly.

"I'm going to tell you more than I told Abuelo, so please. I trust you not to share this with him."

My body tensed. I barely moved my chin while nodding.

"My people have traditions we abide by, and my failure to find a mate means I'm losing certain privileges. Like coming on land—"

"Then find one!" Tears blurred my vision and stung my eyes. I blinked rapidly to stave them off. I'd rather see him taken by another woman than lose his friendship forever. "Why can't you just sweep some girl off of her hooves or something? What if you just decide to come back anyway? What're they gonna do about it? Jail you?"

"Female hippocampi are particularly choosy," he said in a dry voice. "And we have strict laws enforced by my father. He's the alpha, so to speak."

"Laws like what? Laws saying you're not allowed to come back anymore?" I lost my appetite for the star-shaped cuts of pineapple speared to decorative slices of melon. I tossed them and the toothpick aside into a small wastebasket then stared at Dante.

"Because I haven't contributed to the herd, I've been assigned to join the rear guard."

"What the hell is that?"

He held up a hand, begging for me to chill, but I couldn't calm when I was receiving the worst news of the year. My best friend was walking — or swimming, rather — out of my life. I'd never see him again.

"When we follow our migration route, we pass through some dangerous areas that aren't hippocampus friendly. Imagine that you had a group of nomads in the United States, and everywhere the nomads went, marines from the military had to follow because terrorists were hot on their heels."

Terrorists? He must have seen the question in my eyes.

"Sharks. Orcas. Predators of the sea who are larger than us. The rear guard is our military, and we stay behind to fight while the rest of the herd gets away safely."

"Do you guys win most of the time?"

He shook his head. "It depends on the predator. A leopard seal might try to eat a foal, but even the mother can fend them off. I've done it before easily."

"And an orca?"

"Takes about three of us, but someone probably won't swim away."

"Why can't you take a better route if this one is so dangerous? Where the hell do you guys go that it's worth the danger? Kekoa protects the water here and keeps it shark free, but out there…"

"Once we leave this territory and cross the Atlantic, we're in orca territory again. Like I said, they're not so bad. Great whites are our greatest enemy."

"The sharks," I whispered, imagining four massive stallions teaming up beneath the waves to take on a great white. The image made my chest hurt and my eyes water. Nature was rough, I'd known it for years ever since I began studying marine life, but this man was my friend.

"Once we return to our home in the Mediterranean, we're also returning to seas inhabited by sharks. But it's *our* home. We have no other home like it."

"Is it too late to get a mate?"

"No, but it's not going to happen by September. I've accepted that."

"Why don't they want you?" I hugged him tight and set my cheek against his chest. His heartbeat was loud, powerful beneath my ear, a reminder that he hadn't gone yet, that he wasn't a lifeless body floating in some shark's gaping mouth.

Dante wrapped his arms around me. We fit together well, his hugs too comforting over the years.

When I cramped and had PMS, he'd show up with ice cream and sashimi, then we'd curl up on my couch and watch movies into the night together.

When a guy broke my heart, Dante always found out, and he'd listen tirelessly to me as I droned on about how I wished I'd done things differently.

When Dad died last year, Dante had held me throughout the night. He'd packed my bag for me and contacted Teo. My boss flew me home for the funeral on his private jet because Dante asked him to do it.

How long have I been falling in love with him?

"I don't get it," I whispered. "You're a great guy."

"We don't watch movies and do those kinds of things for entertainment out in the ocean, Alessa. I can't impress a filly with my job, my wardrobe, or my music preferences. There, what matters is the color of your fins and whether you've got the most muscles in your tail. The biggest hooves. The fairest mane."

"You have big feet and muscles!"

"I do, and I'm fairly large in my natural state," he confirmed. "But black hair isn't a favorable trait. Dark horses are despised and viewed with scorn. Some of the older hippocampi believe we bring blackness with us wherever we go and cause bad luck."

I tried to imagine him, a sleek fish body attached to a muscled stallion with a jet coat. I pictured wild locks, dark as obsidian, flowing free in the water. The image in my head was beautiful. "Well they're dumb, because I'm sure you're gorgeous." I sniffled and ignored the tears threatening to fall. Dante had seen me at my worst after a breakup, an absolute snotty mess with red-rimmed eyes. I repeated the words he'd told me then, "If they can't see how amazing you are, then they don't deserve to have you."

Dante chuckled weakly as I threw his words back at him. His heart wasn't in it. "You have a good memory."

"You were right." I bit my lower lip. "What if… what if you leave the herd and stay here forever? Isn't defiance better than death?"

He shook his head. "I'd waste away and get sick again. We're not like most shifters who can strike out on their own. A lone wolf can survive without a pack, but we're a magical collective. Together in large numbers, we're stronger. Separated, we weaken. Ask Abuelo about when I was a child. I don't remember much of it, but when my mother died I washed up on the beach and he took care of me like a normal child. I got pretty ill as the months went on."

"What are our choices here, Dante? Maybe you've given up but I'm not going to. There has to be something to do to keep you from becoming shark kibble."

"There's only one option, and I'm reluctant to ask you to help," Dante said. "It's a little extreme."

"I'll be the one to decide that. What would you need from me?"

"A baby."

Our eye contact held during the long silence between us. He didn't look away and neither did I, but my mouth finally fell slack when I realized it wasn't Dante's brand of humor in an attempt to make me laugh.

"Extreme is an understatement," I finally ventured. "A baby is supposed to save you from becoming a snack?"

"If I can produce a child for the herd, then I'll be granted full rights. It's like gaining citizenship."

"What if the baby is human? What if the baby is only half hippocampus?"

"The shifter trait is a strong gene, Alessa. Any child born from a shifter parent is always a shifter, too. So he or she would come with me to the ocean to live with the herd."

My anxiety formed a hard lump in the pit of my belly. My chest tightened, tension creating an invisible cage around my lungs.

This wasn't the typical Dante request. Bumming a buck off of me for a Coke or asking for a ride deep into the mainland was the limit. This was...

"Your baby. You want me to give you a baby I'll never see again?"

I sat down, harder than intended into a rocking bench. It felt unyielding beneath my bottom, the wooden edge pressing into my thighs.

"Don't humans do that all the time? Carry babies for others, or even just give them away?"

I wanted to slap him, but he looked genuinely curious, so I sighed instead. "Not nearly as often as television would have you believe. There are usually special circumstances."

"Is this not special?"

"I need time to think about it. I…"

It meant I'd be having sex with Dante. My mouth became dry, a barren, parched desert where my tongue used to reside. I gazed up at the shirtless man in front of me then let my eyes travel over the heavy muscle comprising his athletic bulk. His broad shoulders, chiseled torso, the washboard abs I'd dreamed of touching for the past two weeks since his return.

It also meant I'd be giving up my first child. Maybe my only child. "I *will* see you both again each year, right?"

"Would you want to?"

I did slap him that time. I was up and on my feet again, my hand flying at his face by reflex before my mind realized I was doing it.

"You're my *friend*. You think I wouldn't want to see you again?" *God, is he really that dense?* Didn't he realize I was always the first to greet him with enthusiastic hugs?

Dante rubbed his reddened cheek. The other blushed hard to match it.

"Your dad is a real prick. The apple doesn't fall far from the tree though if you'd think for one second I want to be without your friendship. I want you safe, but I want you *here*, too."

"Sorry," he said, genuinely apologetic. "I don't expect him to bend the rules for me, though. This is my thirtieth birthday and I've been a drain on the herd long enough."

Silent, I listened to him talk about the herd, their troubles, their dying numbers, and his father's chilliness toward him since his mother's death. By the end, I wanted to weep for my friend and his people. I'd always known Dante had a strained relationship with his dad, but the truth of it made me angry for him.

Letting my chin drop, I considered his request. A child from my womb in exchange for his guaranteed safety. A baby conceived by the two of us to help replenish a dying breed. Could I be that selfless?

"Hey. *Hey.*" His fingers cupped my chin, directing my eyes back to his face. "I don't want you to feel as if you *have* to do this for me. You don't. None of this is your problem, and it was stupid of me to even bring it up."

"Bullshit. You've been thinking about this. You planned things out, Dante. All of this to break some sad news to me about you leaving? You were *hoping* I'd ask if I could help. You arranged this to butter me up and you had Teo's help," I accused.

"I did hope you would ask," he admitted. "But the rest of my statement still stands."

"Why me?" I was afraid of the answer, but I had to know. Was it because I was convenient? Was it some sort of pity play because I was single every summer since we had first met? Did he simply not know anyone else? Or did I seem desperate enough to birth a kid for him and just let it go?

He didn't answer.

"Why me?" I repeated. "Why not Judy? Why not some beach bimbo? Your clients like you enough. You've screwed some of them." More than a few over the years. At least one out of five women taking his classes weren't interested in learning to surf.

Dante remained silent.

"Answer me!"

I had more to say, planning to call him a coward and any other word that came to mind, when Dante shoved me against the wooden beam and pressed his lips over mine.

His tongue plundered my mouth, and then one of his hands slid over my thigh. I let him raise it to his hip, and then without warning, he hoisted me up.

The finesse was lost as our kiss deepened, but he made up for it with raw hunger and his animal instinct. Hints of rum flavored his tongue, delighting me when I gave the tip a playful suckle.

Dante met my flirt with a nudge of his hips, grinding his erection against me with exquisite friction. I nibbled his lower lip and drew back for breath to find his dark blue eyes trained on my face, watching me closely while his chest heaved.

"Whoa." He made me feel feather light, both of his hands on my ass, one palm on each cheek.

"You wanted my reason. That's my reason. Because I've wanted to do that ever since I saw you in the mermaid tank. Because I can't get you out of my fucking mind and you're there all of the time now. Because you've been my best friend, and I thought if I had to go away into the ocean forever and never see you again, I'd want to take some part of you with me." He paused, the look in his eyes so intense I could drown in it. "Because I'm falling in love with you."

I couldn't breathe, but our lips still found each other for a shyer, gentler version of our first kiss. "Okay," I whispered against his mouth.

"Okay what?"

"I'll do it."

I'd have his baby, if it meant he could come back to me again.

Chapter 5

~ALESSA~

I took the rest of the month to consider the gravity of the situation. During those days, we restricted our time to casual outings with our mutual friends but never risked being alone together. The sexual tension between us reached an all-time high when I came within one breath of ripping his clothes off at a beach party. My friends sensed a change in us, which they ignored until I rushed away to wash my face in the bathroom.

"Alessa? Are you okay, sweetie?"

"I'm fine," I called through the door.

Dante's touch inspired the worst kind of thoughts, even a hand to my elbow felt charged with electricity. I'd had to get away before impulsively kissing him became my only option.

"Oh… well, okay," Pam replied.

I didn't want a random case of the hots for his body to influence an important, life-changing decision for both of us. Telling him that was easier said than done. I avoided him altogether for a week, until Julia assumed we were fighting and approached him on the beach to demand to know what he'd done.

"I said you were pissed at me for chasing off her brother then putting myself in your personal business," Dante said over the phone.

"Mm, well. I was a little upset that night. I'm a big girl and I can send off my own shitty ex-boyfriends." I sank deeper into the clawfoot bath tub, enjoying the floral-scented steam drifting up around me.

"I know you can, but it would have been shitty of me to sit there and let him talk to you that way."

"True, I guess. Anyway, I'm sorry she tracked you down like that."

"It's fine. I'm sorry I made everything awkward between us."

Is that how he feels? "You didn't make everything awkward, Dante. What are you talking about?"

"I burdened your conscience with an unfair request."

"Hey, you didn't do anything wrong. This is my choice, remember? Speaking of which, I wanted to let you know I'm ready."

"For what?"

I rolled my eyes even though he couldn't see it. "I'm ready to start on the baby-making," I clarified, enunciating my words.

"Oh."

We made plans to meet in neutral territory at La Flor Rosada, the overpriced resort bar a fifteen-minute walk from my place. If he'd arrived directly on my doorstep, I would have felt compelled to greet him in lingerie and change the entire tone of why we were doing it.

He's not in love with me. He said he's falling in love with me. Big difference. Huge difference, I reminded myself. *We'll work on one thing and let the rest fall into place.*

After the first three outfit changes, I firmly reminded myself we weren't having a date. We weren't going out for dinner and dancing. So I settled on a seafoam green sundress with a built-in bra. The flirty hemline danced around my knees without the risk of flashing my panties to the beach if a wind kicked up.

I arrived first, and while waiting for Dante to join me, I downed two quick shots of tequila for courage. Flora, the bartender and owner, flashed a concerned but gentle smile.

"Is everything okay, señorita? You are not yourself. You talk about it?" she offered.

I shook my head, grimacing through the burn. "No, nothing's wrong, Flora. Thanks."

"Work is stressful. I get it. You have another drink on me." She poured a double shot of tequila and flit to the next customer.

It burned going down, the perfect distraction from my worry.

Dante wandered up five minutes later and took a seat on the stool beside mine. He eyed the empty shot glasses until I nudged the remaining half of my double toward him.

"Saved it for you."

"I meant what I said, Alessa. This isn't… I won't hold it against you if you change your mind. I'd understand." He downed the remainder of the tequila.

"I said I want to do it. I only needed a little time to be one hundred percent certain I'd have no regrets about it."

"All right." He backed off and fell into silence, only to climb off his stool. "Wanna go for a walk first?"

I blinked at him.

"What's with that look?"

"I, uh…" *A walk. Sure, okay, I can do that.*

"Hola, Flora," he called to the bartender. "Add Alessa's drinks to my tab, por favor."

"*Claro que sí.*"

Strong fingers took ahold of my hand, casual like we'd done it a hundred times before. It even felt that way, our hand holding no stranger than the sun descending below the horizon.

"Is this a date?" I impulsively asked as we crossed the beach.

"Did you expect to hop in bed right away?"

Yes. I didn't say the word aloud but my expression answered for me.

"Did you think I'd have my way with you a few times and be done?"

A few times. I shivered and avoided eye contact with him. Pregnancy on the first time only happened to unfortunate virgins and romance novel heroines. I hadn't considered how often we'd meet after consummating our new arrangement. "Maybe," I answered.

"I'm not going to fuck you and leave, unless that's what you want me to do, Alessa."

I shook my head and stole a shy look at him. His attention was on the water, watching the sun's shimmer over the cresting waves. Hand in hand, we watched it together until Dante drew me close.

The kiss was a brief tease, his mouth over my lips, tongue rolling over mine. I tasted the hint of tequila and salt from the bar and then it was over.

"Your place?"

I nodded, mind flying away with possibilities, unspoken promises. The air between us was positively charged with raw desire, and it took all of my restraint to walk at a sedate, unrushed pace beside him.

When we reached my home, the sun had lit the ocean on fire in hues of brilliant gold and ruby. I placed my key in the lock then turned to face him. Without warning, my back was against the wood and strong hands had me by the hips. My tipsiness was fading away but I didn't need the alcohol buzz anymore. Not when he had me pinned against my front door.

"I should claim you right here, since you've given me permission to have you," he murmured against my ear.

Where had my sweet and friendly Dante gone for this sexually-charged beast to take his place? Before I could reply, he drew up the skirt of my dress and his fingers skimmed the edge of my panties, tracing the damp lace.

"Everyone would see," I whispered. A glance to the side revealed my neighbors packing up for an outing on the beach. Marc climbed into the driver's seat and his wife set a picnic basket behind the seats on a sturdy storage shelf.

"Maybe I want them to know you are mine." Dante's nostrils flared on his next breath, making it apparent he smelled my arousal. It turned him on as much as his touch made me wet with longing.

His index finger split my folds and delved inside, penetrating my body to the knuckle. I gasped. *Holy shit.* Part of me wanted to say fuck it all and let him carry through with the promised threat. Molten heat rushed to my core, the muscles squeezing him instinctively and holding to the intruding digit.

He fingered me at my front door, where anyone walking by could see it. With only his large frame between me and any passing onlookers, I felt exposed. Sexy. On fire for him and completely at his mercy. My back arched against the door and my eyes squeezed shut as the tension wound tighter and tighter.

"Dante," I half moaned, my voice sounding like a whine.

"Do you want me to stop?"

"No!" I protested, grabbing frantically at his shoulders.

I was a rubber band close to the breaking point, but a single flick of his thumb against my clit pushed me over the edge. I shattered and came apart, struggling for air, my breath a keening cry against his shoulder.

It felt like the entire world should have known what he was doing, or heard me screaming, but when I finally opened my eyes again, I saw the winding path in front of my house was vacant. My neighbors' dune buggy was absent from their drive, and hell if I knew when they'd left.

A snap sounded between us as he unbuttoned his board shorts.

God, he was serious about fucking me right here. "No, no, no!" I panicked. "Inside, Dante. The bed. Please."

Before I could utter another word, we were inside and he was tossing me onto my bed. My undignified sprawl had my skirt bunched up around my waist and the spaghetti straps hanging off my shoulders. Dante's eyes roved over me as I peeled my dress down and pushed it past my hips. The rumpled cotton ended up on the floor.

He shrugged off his unbuttoned shirt and let the garment drop to the floor. His board shorts followed.

Oh. My. God.

Dante was long and thick like I'd imagined, surpassing my expectations. The upward curve of his heavy erection revealed a glistening tip, slick with precum. My mouth watered for it, but the survivalist in me thought I'd suffocate trying to blow him.

He's a water horse and he's hung like a horse. Oh, God, what am I getting myself into? How is all of that going to fit into me? To calm myself, I had to let the giggles out.

Dante lowered one knee to the bed between my spread thighs. His dick swayed with the movement before he paused. "What's so funny?"

The dark hair surrounding his cock was soft and silky to my exploring fingers, rather than coarse and curly. "It's nothing. I've just, uh, never been with anyone so large."

I wrapped my fingers around his thick shaft, measuring the girth. My index and thumb didn't touch — I'd always used it as a measure of how large my boyfriends compared to one another.

Dante was the most impressive by far.

At first, a smug grin spread across his face. The expression faded when I gave his dick a teasing pump, gliding my hand down to his base and up to the tip again. Without a word he tugged my panties down my legs. He didn't move again.

"Dante?"

Blue eyes studied me, inspiring every self-conscious thought I'd ever had when falling into bed with a guy. Were my breasts too small? Did he hate the handful of silver marks crawling over my too wide hips? Or was he loathing the wax job and close trim grooming my fiery red curls into a perfect triangle?

"Your ass isn't fat," he said suddenly, heat in his voice.

"Huh?"

"You believed the jackass when he said it. But I'm telling you, he was wrong." His mouth lowered to my hip bone and set me aflame with unabashed desire.

Anticipation welled in my belly as Dante continued his journey across my thigh, nibbling as he moved closer to the middle. Just as I thought he intended to bury his face between my legs, he veered off. Small kisses touched my hip then he nipped me playfully.

"There isn't one part of your body that isn't perfect, Alessa. Thank you."

A day ago, I'd been terrified, expecting awkward sex, silence, and failure to make eye contact. Instead, I felt the same tenderness and affection between us, translating easily from platonic friendship into sensuality.

"You don't have to thank me, Dante."

The blunt tip of him tested my entrance, easing into my body's grip with one inch then another. I trembled.

"Don't tease me," I groaned.

"I'm not teasing," he grunted back. He stilled momentarily and set his weight above me on one arm. "Are you... sure you're not a virgin?"

"What? No!"

Dante relaxed visibly, but sweat beaded at his brow. I raised one hand to run my thumb over his gleaming temple. As a personal reminder, I told myself he was huge, and while I was definitely wet enough, I'd never had a man as well-endowed as him. "It's been a while, but I'm not a virgin. Why?"

"You're so tight."

"You're so big," I teased back once I found my courage to flirt. "And... I want to feel every inch of you." My breath shuddered in and out. "Just do it. I won't break."

Dante slammed home with one fluid stroke. We fit together perfectly as if by design, my body stretched to accommodate every hard inch. My new lover smothered my ragged moan with a kiss then fell into an even, vigorous tempo.

His movements didn't allow time to adjust to the new intrusion. He made a slick backstroke then thrust forward anew, bumping me upward on the bed. The comforter bunched and wrinkled beneath my naked back then his body stretched over mine. The friction of my stiffened nipples against his chest made me writhe beneath him.

"You feel so good," he growled against my ear. "Tell me it's the same for you."

I could barely think, let alone speak, distracted as another toe-curling stroke made stars burst behind my eyes. I ran my fingers up and down his back, feeling the muscles rippling beneath his bronzed skin.

"Tell me, Alessa," he ordered. "Tell me what you want."

"H-harder."

"Lessa…"

"I can take it. I *like* it hard."

He withdrew until only the crowned tip remained, leaving me woefully empty, craving him.

"Dan—" He snapped forward again, filling me, gone, then back once more, hammering my body until the bed rattled against the wall behind my head. I arched beneath him and cried out, thrusting my breasts toward his descending mouth.

No man had ever touched me so deeply, and with each bang of his tip against the back of my walls, there was a sense of undeniable satisfaction amidst fleeting hints of discomfort. We moved together in a frenzied fervor, bodies colliding in splendid rhythm.

"Yes!" I encouraged. He released my nipple with a soft pop, exposing it to the cool bedroom air. He moved to the next, repeated his tease, and traced the tip with his tongue.

His hips rocked to mine over and over, amazing me with his stamina. His tireless endurance. Just as he brought me to the brink, Dante circled his hips and struck me somewhere new, soaring me higher towards bliss.

"Dante, don't stop, don't stop, baby." Tension coiled throughout my entire frame, a slow build he stoked with each powerful press into my hot depths.

My orgasm outside didn't hold a candle to this one. The spasms started small, little firecracker sparks that crackled through my veins to every limb. The slow burn erupted into an inferno, pleasure seizing me in its grasp. As my core clenched around his cock, trapped in the throes of orgasm, Dante muttered against my cheek. He jerked, and then a telltale pulse throb preceded his heat flowing into me.

I tightened my thighs and dug my heels into his ass, wanting him deeper, needing more of him. Dante reached beneath my thigh and bent the knee to my chest. The change of angle and increased depth took me by surprise, bringing delicious friction against my sensitive clit. He grinded desperately, fucking through our mutual climax until I came again. Ecstasy rocketed through straight to the tips of my curling toes.

The noises coming from me sounded inhuman, unrecognizable to my own ears. He silenced them with a kiss until the sensation overcame him as well. We breathed each other's air, our passionate cries mingling as one until we both stilled.

Dante lingered atop me long after his cock went flaccid, though it remained within my body. He pushed up, bracing his weight on both elbows, and peered down at me. With our faces close, I gazed into his blue eyes and smoothed the dark hair from his brow.

Words couldn't convey how I felt, so I said nothing at all. We shared gentle touches, soft kisses, and lingering caresses as we cuddled against the sheets.

We didn't need sex talk and flirtations promising more; actions said everything for us.

Sleep pulled Dante under first, leaving me wide awake beside him, blissfully spent and sore, but too keyed up to close my eyes and rest. I watched his chest move up and down then trailed my fingers over his pecs. The fine dark hair was soft beneath my fingers, his muscles firm, every inch of him absolute perfection.

My Dante. Mine. I don't want to lose him. I don't want to lose this now that I have it. Maybe we're doing things out of order, maybe it's reckless, but I want this so bad.

I wiped the tears from my cheeks and curled up against him, resting one arm across his body. I no longer wanted to give him a baby; I wanted it to be our child to raise together. Somehow, there had to be a way to make my hopes a reality.

When exhaustion finally came, my dreams were of an infant with his blue eyes.

***

I awakened to the aroma of bacon grease and butter. Dante, naked in my kitchen, stood at the stove with a spatula while cooking breakfast.

"Aren't you brave. Not afraid of stray oil pops?" I asked.

"Nope. Get back into bed."

"Back into bed? But you're almost done."

"I wanted to bring you breakfast in bed."

My rumbling belly protested his orders, but I moved from the kitchen to the bedroom. The floor was cool under my feet, my personal air conditioning unit limited to the bedroom only. I gratefully slid into bed and into the vacant spot left by his body. It was warm and smelled like Dante, of the ocean and surf. Nestling against it, I inhaled his scent with my eyes shut until approaching footsteps signaled his return.

He carried in a tray loaded with my best dishes. A single blush-colored orchid claimed my only vase. Where the hell did he get an orchid when there wasn't a single flower in my house and he was still naked?

"Aren't you going to eat?" I asked.

He shook his head. "I don't eat bacon, remember?"

"You got up to make breakfast for only me?"

My plate was massive, the serving size double what I'd normally consume. He'd neatly arranged four fried eggs beside six slices of bacon. Two pieces of buttered toast glistened beneath a generous spread of passion fruit jelly.

The uncertain smile on his face diminished until a frown tugged at the corners of his mouth. "What did I do wrong?"

"Nothing," I said, quick to assuage his worries. "This is great. A lot, but great."

"You are eating for two."

For a moment I stared at him, then I burst out into giggles. "Wow, you really don't know much about making babies, do you?"

Dante stared at me and folded his arms over his chest. His flawless, wondrously sculpted chest. My eyes homed in on it and lost focus on until he spoke up again. "Enlighten me."

"Well, for starters, even if you did manage to knock me up the first time, I don't have to eat for two, as you say, until I'm a little further in."

"This is our breeding season. Before males even mate to their fillies, they fatten them as much as possible," he explained. "Then if food is scarce during the journey home, their milk won't decrease and we won't risk losing the newly-birthed foals."

"No need to worry about food scarcity here." I beamed at him. "We have McDonalds on the island. I'm going to have a Big Mac pregnancy."

My joke coaxed a smile to his face. "And overpriced mahi mahi burgers," he said.

I ate as much as I could, stuffing myself on the crispy bacon then licking my fingers clean.

"That was delicious."

"I'm glad you enjoyed it."

I carried my own dishes to the sink despite his attempts to fuss over me. Over the course of our friendship, he'd spent countless nights at my place, but he'd never tried to serve me like a naked manservant. I wished he had. It would have bloated his ego if he knew I mourned the loss of the years I could have had him standing by as an oiled cabana boy bringing me tea and chocolates.

"So are you free for dinner tonight?" I asked when I caught him stepping into his discarded board shorts in the bedroom.

"I'm booked this evening."

"Oh." I bit my bottom lip and fiddled with my alarm clock. I wasn't due to return to work until Monday and had hoped to spend the entire weekend with him.

"But I can cancel."

"No, don't do that." I forced a smile to my face and leaned up to kiss his cheek. "Do you want your shirt back?" His blue and white, Hawaiian print shirt fit me like a gown, reaching my mid-thigh.

"Nah. Don't need it for private surf lessons."

I controlled my expression, but I couldn't control the red-hot torrent of jealousy scorching through me. With a forced smile, I nodded and trailed with him to the door. "Tomorrow then?"

"Sure."

I waited for him to kiss me, but it never came. Dante hugged me, ran his fingers through my sleep-tousled hair, and stepped outside onto the porch. "Relax today, Alessa. You earned some rest, and I'll catch you tomorrow."

Relax. Right. Like I'll get any of that done while last night's events play through my mind on repeat.

Chapter 6

~ALESSA~

In hindsight, I realized it was stupid to make plans for a weekend with a guy without discussing those plans first. But it didn't change how much I wished he'd kissed me goodbye.

"I thought you were going to be busy this weekend?" Pam said.

With our employee ID badges in hand, we meandered through aisles at one of the island's shopping centers. On his resort, Teo was practically king of his own empire — giving his tourists and employees access to restaurants of varying price, shopping centers, and even a solar-powered electric rail system for transportation. Whenever we tired of his beach paradise, we took the scheduled ferry boat to the mainland.

"Yeah, well, things fell through," I grumbled. Plucking a box of chocolates from the shelf, I added it to my basket. "He served me breakfast then took off."

"Wait. He?" Julia peered over. Both friends stared me down with matching expressions of disbelief. "You didn't say your plans involved a guy!"

"Doesn't matter now, he's busy today and it was dumb to assume he'd want to hang out." After a peek at my thighs, I put the chocolates back on the shelf. Julia tucked it into my basket again with a second box.

"You spent all night bouncing on some man. You need this for your strength. No wonder you're dragging ass all over like you didn't sleep."

Another customer at the end of the aisle glanced at us. The gray-haired old woman quickly scurried to the next row. Heat flooded to my cheeks as I turned to swat my friend. "Can't you lower your voice, megaphone mouth?"

"Sorry, chica. Anyway, tell us about this guy and his breakfast skills." Julia looked far from apologetic.

"I'm not giving you details. Suffice to say, we had a good time and he fries up a great plate of bacon and eggs. I woke up to him cooking in the buff and then he shooed me back to bed so he could bring a tray in. Orchid, linen napkin, and all that fancy stuff like you see in movies."

"Wait, wait, wait. You're saying this guy brought you breakfast in bed, naked I might add, and a flower too?" Pam asked.

"Yeah, he did." I still didn't know where the hell he'd gotten a flower while naked. My neighbors must have gotten quite the show.

"And he spent all night banging you like a pair of bongos?" Julia asked.

"Yeah."

"But was there in the morning still to make you this breakfast in bed," Pam clarified.

"I just said yes."

"He likes you. Why are you freaking out?"

"I dunno, I just…" I shrugged, at a loss. *How do I explain the irrational jealousy?* "He was all keen to rush away for lessons and stuff and I guess I expected him to have the weekend off like I do."

"It's Dante, isn't it?" Pam blurted out.

"No!" I lied through my teeth, denying it too quickly.

"Oh my God, it is. You slept with Dante, you little heifer. How was it?"

"I knew you two were gonna do it eventually," Julia said. "This doesn't surprise me at all."

I sighed and twirled a few strands of red hair around my index finger. "It was incredible, but I thought we'd spend the entire weekend together, you know? Why book lessons in advance if he knew we were gonna—" I stopped, abruptly halting myself.

"Wait. If he knew you were gonna…?"

"Go out," I offered up in a quick cover. If anyone would understand my decision to have a baby for Dante, it would be Julia and Pam. Only a few months ago, they'd decided to undergo sperm donation and save money to raise a child of their own.

"He's a man, hon. We already established they're not the best planners," Pam said.

"Besides, you two have been dancing around each other for years. It's about time you both took the plunge."

If only they knew how deep. I forced a smile and pushed my uneasiness aside. "You're right. There's nothing to worry about."

"I knew you two were meant for each other ever since the first time he fawned over you and your mutant lungs," Julia said.

I laughed quietly. "I don't have mutant lungs. Holding my breath for a long time isn't anything special."

We finished our shopping and decided to follow the beach route back toward our residences. Crowds were thinner in spring than during the summer, but everything was open, including our favorite little fish hut. Dante's grandfather fished every morning and served up his daily catch.

"Afternoon, Abuelo," we all greeted in unison.

"Buenas tardes, señoritas," he offered in return, a perpetual smile on his aging face. I was glad to see him on his feet again working the stall — it wasn't the same without him on the beach.

Our matching orders of fish and plantain chips arrived within ten minutes. The perfect amount of sweetness, spice, and chili dust warmed my mouth when I took the first bite of deep-fried goodness. Abuelo refused to share his secret batter recipe, no matter how many times I begged or tried to bribe him with candies.

When I found him over the winter, he made me promise to keep it to myself. I helped the old man to the ferry, then we drove to the nearest hospital. He hadn't wanted anyone to know he was ill.

I'd visited him every day, wondering why he didn't phone relatives or even call Dante. Now I knew why. Cell phone reception wouldn't reach the ocean floor.

"Gracias," I chirped to him. I leaned forward and kissed his cheek. Abuelo would be missed one day, not only for his fish, but for his sense of humor and terrible jokes.

This plan has to work. Dante should be here with him. And me!

"Oh look, no wonder you wanted to come this way. There's Dante now." Pam nudged me in my ribs as we walked down the beach with our food.

"It was Julia's suggestion, remember?" But I hadn't argued against it, hoping to see him. I regretted listening to her.

Dante had his hands on the hips of one of the resort's regulars, a middle-aged woman with a big fat diamond on her left hand who always came without her husband. He coaxed her through the proper stance while she stood on a surfboard laid out on the sand. The woman's barely there bikini wasn't great surf attire.

"You know, I don't think I've ever seen Mrs. Courtland actually get on a board in the water," Pam pointed out.

"As much money as she throws at lessons she should be a pro," I griped.

"His job could be worse. With that body he could give Channing Tatum a run for his money and be in the next Magic Mike," Julia said.

I grimaced. "Yeah. Point." At least he was clothed. Somewhat. The sun gleamed over his tanned limbs and toned back, highlighted by the sweat glistening on every muscle.

"Don't worry about it, sweetie. They're always throwing themselves at him." Julia rubbed my arm.

"I'm not upset," I lied, failing to conceal my forlorn expression.

"You are, but it's okay to be a little upset. Come on. We have a Netflix marathon to watch and we're dragging you along for the ride."

Wine, chocolates, and movies. It sounded like the makings for a perfect girls' night in.

***

I writhed beneath him, our legs tangled in the sheets, his heavier bulk a warm blanket over my healthy curves. Dante's lips were the perfect cure for a sleepless night, his hands the only remedy for my insomnia. With one hard thrust, he claimed me and slid to meet the perfect depth.

"Do you know how much I need you?" he whispered against my lips.

My answer escaped in a groan. My body trembled, captive by the frenetic rhythm of his thrusts, his balls slapping against me. On the brink of climax, I buried my nails into his back and gasped his name as he drove forward again.

Riiiiing.

My dream hottie evaporated. The only thing sprawled over me was a rumpled blanket. A dream. He hadn't visited me that night to apologize for his abrupt exit, and my wild imagination had worked my body up to a feverish state of excitement in his place.

Riiiiing.

"Crap!" I dove for the phone on the bedside table and plucked it from the cradle. "Hello?"

"Hi, Alessa! Did I wake you?" My mother's cheerful voice spilled from the phone.

I blearily rubbed my eyes and squinted at the digital clock. A quarter to ten. "Yeah, but I was about to get up soon anyway." I crawled from the bed and onto my feet.

I wished a call from my mother was enough to douse cold water on my arousal, but it wasn't. It only made the phone call awkward instead. Slick and wet with my need, I peeled off my damp panties and tossed them into the laundry bin.

"If it's a bad time I can call back," she offered, sensing my distress. "I wanted to let you know my flight is booked for the summer."

"Huh? Flight? What flight? Where are you going?"

"To visit you, silly."

Her announcement took me by surprise.

"Mom! You could have at least let me know so I could get you a room on my employee discount," I wailed over the line. Reservations usually came at a three month *minimum*.

"I didn't want you to spend your money on me, sweetheart. I'll just stay with you again. I thought it would be nice to finally see the island in the summer, even if it is the busy tourist season. Don't worry. I won't interrupt your work. I can fend for myself and enjoy the sights."

"It's not my money. It's a discount," I rationalized.

A fist pounded against my front door. I pivoted on a foot and moved into the main room, my modest couch and television the reason I hated the idea of putting mom up at my place. A glance through the windows revealed Dante on my porch.

With her in town, our baby-making plans would have to be put on the backburner if I wasn't pregnant by the time she arrived.

"Hey Mom, I gotta go. Someone from work is here. Email me your details, okay?"

"Sounds good, sweetie. I'll see you soon."

I disconnected the call and pulled open the door. "Hey," I greeted, my voice breathy. Dante wore his usual, board shorts and an unbuttoned top. Today it was a solid peach color he pulled off without any loss to his masculinity.

"Morning, Alessa."

We studied each other in silence, each waiting for the other to talk. He didn't invite himself in, and I didn't offer.

"I tried to call you last night," I said quietly.

"I had something to take care of." His eyes dropped to the phone in my hand then crept up my t-shirt clothed body. Thin cotton failed to disguise my nipples, but the weight of his gaze on them restored the hot longing inspired by my dream. I tugged self-consciously on the hem. "Should I come back later?"

"Oh, no, come on in. Did you need something?"

"Yes." He stepped inside, nudging me back by his sheer presence, and pulled the door shut behind him. "You."

"Whoa, hold up a second buster." I threw both hands up and pushed at his chest. His perplexed expression might have been funny if I wasn't so incredibly insulted. "You don't get to show up for sex whenever you feel like it. I'm not your personal fuck-puppet."

"You agreed—"

"I agreed to carry your baby, yes. It still doesn't mean you get to hit me up for sex and bounce back to your beach bunnies."

Dante's expression fell, washed away as if I'd splashed him with ice water. "Alessa—"

"Don't 'Alessa' me," I fired back at him. "I'm still going to do this." Because the idea of motherhood had gained momentum, like a speeding mack truck with blown brake lines. "And I haven't changed my mind, but I'll be damned if…" I inhaled deeply and took time to gather my thoughts. Dante watched me in silence without interrupting again. "I need to know, Dante. Are you still sleeping around with the guests?"

"Why would you ask that?"

"I saw you yesterday during Mrs. Courtland's lesson and I know, for the past three years, she's slipped you her room key. We all know."

"So? It doesn't mean I've ever made a visit to her room," he bit back at me. "Is that how little faith you have in me?"

"Oh come on, Dante, you've screwed plenty of girls. You're hot and you're single, so it's not like it's a big deal."

"I haven't slept with a client in two seasons," Dante said. "Not last season. Not this season. Not once."

A sick feeling churned in my gut, lying beneath the fleeting sense of elation. "No one last year or this year?"

"No one."

But me.

He took my hands gently, dwarfing them with his larger fingers. "We don't have to do this, Alessa. Asking you to birth a child for me put you in a shitty position. Let's forget it. The last thing I want is for you to feel used in *any* way. Leaving this island with your friendship matters more to me… than… than anything," he confessed.

I shook my head. "No, I'm being dumb. I guess it hurt my feelings when you walked out yesterday. I'd just thought…"

"I offered to cancel," he reminded me, a fact forgotten while I sniveled in my pity party.

"And I should have graciously accepted."

He raised my hand to his mouth and kissed my fingers, sending electric tingles across my skin.

"I'm sorry. For assuming the worst about last night," I whispered.

"I have a gift for you."

I blinked. "You didn't have to do that."

Dante smiled. "I know, but I wanted to." Releasing my hands first, he pulled open the velcro flap over his pocket and reached inside.

A gorgeous necklace glittered in the sunbeams filtering through my living room window. Pearls and small shells hung on gold wire, forming an elegant piece suitable for an underwater princess. A multi-hued scallop shell dangled at the center, red streaked with orange and cream.

"Dante, this is *beautiful*," I squealed once I found my voice.

"True mermaids wear something similar," he said. "You resemble one."

Dante fastened his gift around my neck, pressing a kiss against my nape before he stepped back. The central pendant hung right above the hollow of my breasts. Nothing in my jewelry box compared to the unique piece, which meant...

"You made this for me?"

He nodded. "I searched the ocean floor after rebuffing Mrs. Courtland. I wanted to find something special for you."

I pictured him awake throughout the night hunting down little shells. Suddenly, the vast amount of pearls and polished stones in his grandfather's inventory made sense. Dante found them. He found all of them. "Thank you. It's the loveliest thing anyone's ever given me," I whispered with my chin low. It was too pretty to look away.

"Should I leave now?"

"No. Please stay. We should talk anyway." With my hand in his, I guided him to the couch then fetched glasses of passion fruit juice from the fridge. He tried to coax me onto his lap, but I settled beside him instead, hoping to conceal my lack of panties.

"I still want to do this, Dante, but I think we need to clear some things up," I said.

"I'm listening." He plucked at the hem of my t-shirt, having a look before I could swat his hand away.

Damn. He saw. "So, while your, uh, alpha male thing is sorta hot, you can't just show up whenever you feel like it for a quickie."

"Who said it would have been quick?" Dante grinned.

Double damn.

Obviously quickie wasn't in his vocabulary. Sometime later, deep into the afternoon, he had reduced me to a sweaty and limp pile of uselessness. Sprawled facedown on my bed with Dante stretched out beside me, I was reminded of my dream. He stroked his warm hand over my back while I drifted in and out of consciousness. Each time I dozed off I startled awake, only to find he was still beside me.

"My willpower is weak," I mumbled against the pillow. "I was going to resist you."

Dante peppered kisses across my shoulders. "Come out with me for a swim. I want to make it up to you for yesterday."

"I can't even move off the bed and you want to swim?" I laughed and managed to flop over onto my back. "Besides, I think I'm supposed to lay here and let your guys have their chance. Tomorrow?"

"I'll give you an hour."

"Masochist."

Dante leaned down and kissed me. "I'll settle for a movie at IMAX, but tomorrow, you have to let me put you on a board."

Noooooooo, I thought. "I don't have the balance for that!

"You're in luck because I happen to be an excellent teacher."

Chapter 7

~DANTE~

I looked forward to every passing moment with Alessa. We visited each other every day and made love frequently, but I could never kiss her enough to sate the ache she created in my heart.

The inner stallion in me wanted more than sensual matings in her bed, and every time I caught her performances at the mermaid tank, the drive to claim her grew more irresistible.

I didn't know how long I could last. How long I'd have the restraint to keep the wild beast in me at bay. The past weeks had been both heaven and hell, worsened when she revealed our first attempt at pregnancy ended in failure. With no alternative, we tried again.

"How do you know she doesn't want it?" Teo asked me. Swimming no longer distracted me from the pressing need to make Alessa mine, so I'd abandoned my trunks and weighed them to the bottom of the ocean with a rock before hurrying to Teo's island. My father's useless proclamations rang in my ears, making me desperate for advice from a man who would understand.

Feline eyes peered at me from the thick foliage bordering the garden where we chatted. Teo's free range jaguars always kept out of sight whenever I visited; I hadn't yet earned their trust. Or they were waiting for me to let down my guard to eat me. I hoped it was the former.

Bright pink hibiscus bloomed from several bushes and the sweet smell of orchids floated on the balmy afternoon breeze. Behind us, a hot spring pool gently bubbled. Teo's home was an island paradise.

"While you have the privilege of living beside your mate every day of the year, I'm not so fortunate, Teo. I'll be away in the ocean half of our lives. No woman wants that."

"Allow her to make her own decision," Teo insisted. "A smart woman knows what she wants, and Alessa is no exception."

Teo's mate arrived bearing a tray in her hands. The voluptuous human woman wore a scarlet sundress, neatly coiffed black waves against her bare shoulders. For her comfort, Teo and Kekoa kept spare clothes around for shapeshifting visitors. I wore a modest pair of board shorts and a big smile when the scent of sugar and vanilla reached my nose.

"Are you boys hungry?"

"Cookies?" Teo straightened in his seat, resembling an eager school child.

"I couldn't help but overhear the conversation but…" Marcy bit her lower lip. "I think my husband is right this time. This rare, singular time," she repeated for emphasis while lowering a plate of still warm cookies in front of the dragon. He sulked until she set the glass of milk beside them.

"Where is Javier?" I twisted around and searched for their little boy. I'd given the child a ride in the water a week ago and found myself longing even more for a foal of my own. I hoped for a little colt with Alessa's gray eyes.

"Down for his nap," Marcy replied. "Otherwise he'd be out here eating all the cookies with his daddy. Don't worry, I saved him some."

"In that case." I helped myself to several cookies from the plate. They were warm and gooey, filled with cheesecake and caramel centers. The sweet delights melted on my tongue.

"Anyway." Marcy ran her fingers over Teo's hair, combing her slim digits through his shoulder-length waves. "You men need to trust us to know what we want sometimes. Don't make decisions without consulting with us."

I washed down a couple more cookies with my glass of milk. "How long has it been since you both became mated?"

"Nearly ten years now," Marcy said happily. Teo swept the woman into his lap and fed her a cookie. They were the definition of contentment, the kind of peace any shifter would aspire to possess for himself.

"I have no regrets about the path our lives have taken together," Teo said.

I wanted a semblance of his life for my own. Hours later, when leaving their home after dinner, the ocean raised my hopeless spirits and carried me toward the resort. Thoughts of Alessa weighed heavily on my mind, along with my inner beast's yearning to make her mine and to be owned by her in return.

***

My stallion's possessive and jealous nature made attending Alessa's shows unsafe for the people around me. For the third time in a row, I missed her performance, but this time, I had a damned good reason. A surprise for her. The girls all squealed when I cracked the dressing room door open to shout inside.

"Keep your swimsuit on, Alessa! We have plans!"

"Dante!" She popped into view and squeezed outside to shove her palm against my chest. The color flushing her cheeks matched her hair. "Do you *mind*, pervert?"

"I didn't step *inside*," I grumbled. "I didn't think you'd hear me through the door."

"I would have heard you loud and clear."

My eyes swept over her body, lush curves, thick thighs, and rounded hips perfect for childbearing. The green bikini bottom snugly clung to her fair skin. I hardened in seconds.

"Maybe I couldn't wait to see you."

"Maybe you need to learn to wait a few minutes," she shot back. Her voice softened and a smile crept onto her face. "Why do I need my suit on?"

"Because, despite how much I'd like you to be without it right now, I want to introduce you to some of my friends." I set my hands on her hips and squeezed, enjoying the pliable flesh beneath my fingers.

"We have most of the same friends, Dante."

"No. *My* friends."

When the understanding dawned on Alessa's face, her mouth formed a small 'o' of surprise. "Let me grab my stuff then."

After a stop by her house for her to dump her belongings and fetch her digital camera, we headed down to the dock and borrowed Teo's spare boat. He'd given us permission to meet on the cove at his personal island. Less than a half hour later, we reached Teo's dock and I moored the boat in place.

"You ready?"

"I'm not sure. Do they know you're bringing a human?"

"They know everything about you," I confirmed.

Alessa shot me a skeptical look then we made our way onto the wooden dock and across the sand. With her camera secured in an expensive, waterproof case, she'd hoped to capture the afternoon with us magical creatures in digital form.

I'd never allowed anyone to photograph me before, but I knew my father would flip his shit if he found out.

Screw him, I seethed internally. *Let her take a hundred photos.*

"Dante? You okay?"

"Hm?"

"You looked…" She gestured helplessly with a hand, a worried expression causing her lips to press together in a thin line. "Upset."

"I'm fine."

"No, you're n—mmph."

I kissed her, hard. Pressing my fingers against her ass, holding her tight against me, letting her feel the hard-on she could inspire with only a kiss. Thinking about my father dampened the mood, but being with her chased away his unjust expectations. I palmed one full breast and slipped my hand between it and the bikini triangle cupping her flesh. She moaned into my mouth, question forgotten and her lust unmistakable.

Breaking the kiss, I turned my lips to her throat and skimmed my mouth down the slender column. "They don't have clothes. Is that okay with you?"

"Okay, so cove full of naked hotties. Gotcha. Oh, yeah… fine with me," she breathed out."

I pinched her nipple, earning another quiet moan. "Can you remember that we won't hurt you?" Alessa's body was so damned responsive I couldn't stop touching her, and skin to skin contact had become an addiction.

"I trust you, and if they're your friends, I trust them... but..." She trailed her fingers over my cock. The hard length jumped beneath her fingers and eagerly twitched. "We're never going to make it to the cove if you keep doing this."

"I'll stop," I said, chagrined. The guys would beat me to the bottom of the ocean and bury my corpse in the sand if I didn't make good on my promise to let them meet an actual human. One of them had no experience whatsoever with his human body, but they were all eager, as if *she* were the mythical creature that belonged in fairy tales.

Somehow, I managed to cool off along the walk to the cove. With her hand in mine, she chattered about the show, how well the female audience members responded to the addition of two mermen, and how much she'd secretly missed playing the part of the mermaid princess.

"Alessa?"

"Hmm?"

"There's something I want to try, and I know it's going to sound crazy to you."

"Is this a baby making thing? I told you not to get discouraged. My period isn't due again for another week so we'll know soon."

"No. It's not about that exactly. Loosely related but not entirely."

Alessa peered up at me. "What then?"

"I want to…" Licking my lips nervously, I searched for the words to voice my desires. "I want to make you mine, but if you accept it, it's kind of a one-way road for me."

"Yours?"

"It's a soul bond meant for mates, like the mark on Marcy's shoulder."

"She told me he bit her." Alessa raised one hand to her bare shoulder and touched the flawless skin. "Would you bite me there, too?"

I shook my head. "No. We don't bite. That's a dragon thing."

"And she said it's like being married. So… are you asking me to marry you?"

My heart hammered against my chest. "In the only way my kind do it, yes."

Alessa was quiet for the next few steps, her expression contemplative. "So, how does it work?"

"I've never done it, but everyone says it comes naturally once the beast takes over."

"Do you mind if I think on it for a little while? I mean, in case I have something else I want to ask you about it?"

"Of course," I replied. The last thing I wanted was to rush her. "Look, I see Hyrum and Lycus. They're both a little unfamiliar with their human bodies, so you'll have to excuse them if they don't greet you on two legs."

"How many friends are coming? You never said."

"Hyrum and Lycus are on the rear guard with me, but Zeno and Helena are mated."

A worried expression flickered across her face. "She's not going to hate me for stealing you away from the herd is she?"

"Oh no. Most mares are friendly," I explained. "They may be choosy, but they're not unkind. These two would have brought their foal, but they're unsure of you."

"A foal…" She gazed dreamily at the water, clutching the Nikon resting against her abdomen. It dangled from the black nylon strap secured around her neck. "I see them!"

Four equine heads rose from the waves, leading powerful frames made for cutting effortlessly through the waves. Hyrum, a six-year veteran of the rear guard, fearlessly came ashore first. Like me, his pelt was in darker shades, but dappled gray and black swirled with hints of white.

Alessa squealed and adjusted her camera lens. It clicked, focused, clicked, and focused anew with each photo of the hippocampi emerging from the ocean. "Oh my God. He looks like a horse! Like a stallion with fins! Are these flippers or hooves? What do you call them? Can I touch him?" She whirled to face me. "Is it okay to touch him? Is that breaking a rule?"

I translated her request to Phoenician then my bold friend moved across the sand on his flippers. Our hooves varied from our land counterparts. Instead, they flattened out into a webbed, flipper shape to help us propel in the water. Lacking hind legs, his barrel-shaped equine ribcage tapered to a scaled, sapphire blue fishtail packed with muscle. Hyrum lacked a dorsal fin, and for that reason, he'd been found unsuitable for mating by our eligible fillies.

While the other three hung in the shallow surf, he marched up to her and dipped his head in respect.

"He's telling you it's okay."

A trembling hand raised to touch the black fur covering Hyrum's equine face. The stallion remained still, taking my warning to heart. I'd told them all she was shy and had never met a supernatural creature before up close and personal except for the island's owner.

Then Zeno had demanded to know why I'd never let her see me.

Because I'm terrified. Because if she sees the real me, that I'm a sea monster, she won't want me anymore. I'll lose her.

"His fur feels like sealskin... Oh my God, oh my God." Alessa repeated herself over and over while running her fingers over Hyrum's mane. He soaked up the attention while I watched, jealous and wanting to be in his place instead.

Maybe she can love me and see I'm still her *Dante under all the fur and scales.*

"He's magnificent. Thank you." Alessa's smile lit up her entire face. Watching her flooded my heart with joy and an undeniable urge to throw off my clothes and show her my stallion form.

Zeno and Helena moved from the water next, shiftomg mid-stride and joining hands. Helena's body brought to mind photos of old renaissance paintings I'd viewed online while surfing the internet. Like Aphrodite in the *Birth of Venus*, she had thick thighs and a soft stomach beneath two pert breasts. Waist-length strawberry blonde hair slicked behind her shoulders, and like most mares, she easily stood six feet tall while on legs.

Helena waved shyly and Zeno watched us from beside his mate. He was nearly six and a half feet tall, solid and muscular with a frame like an American footballer. Lycus moved up alongside them in his human body, his chestnut hair hanging wetly around his shoulders. Smaller than the rest of us guys, he'd gone his entire adult life without attention from the fillies in our herd. At least they'd flirted with me and shown me attention.

"They don't speak much English," I told Alessa. "But I can translate anything you want to say."

"Is that why you won't show me your horse, too? Cause you have to translate?"

She *wanted* to see? "Er… That wasn't why."

"Well? Are you going to let me see you then?"

"Do you want to?"

Alessa nodded and tightly clutched her camera. "More than anything."

Slipping my thumbs into the waistband of my shorts, I shoved them down and stepped free. The prompt transformation overtook me, contorting the bones of a human body into the frame of a seahorse. My muscles grew and my spine elongated. A sharp arc of short-lived, exquisite pain shot through me.

Alessa stared at me, her bright eyes large in her oval face. In my animal form, every sense became amplified except for my eyesight. My field of vision broadened at the cost of including blind spots I didn't have as a human. I tilted my head to watch her approach, wanting to see her for every second.

Tears shimmered in her eyes. "You're… exactly as I saw you in my dream." Elation filled me at the first stroke to my face, then she kissed my nose. Curious fingers threaded through my black mane and slid over the ink-colored fur covering my upper body. I stood still as she moved around me to my hindquarters where a sleek fishtail lay over the damp sand.

"Your color is amazing. I knew you'd be beautiful but…." Her voice trailed. "Do I get to ride you?"

No human rode a hippocampus. It was a tradition long ended when my ancestors retreated from their former Phoenician masters and we were lost to myths and legends. We were all friends once — now we hid from humanity.

Flattening my body to the gritty sand, I lowered so Alessa could swing one leg over my back. The others watched with mixed expressions, curiosity and bewilderment.

With Alessa secure, I dragged my body into the surf and kept to the surface. She laughed, a delighted sound that warmed my heart. She wasn't afraid. Wasn't repulsed. I sped through the water, salty spray lifting into the air.

"I can't believe I'm actually doing this," Alessa cried out with a peal of laughter. "Can you take me under?"

I hesitated before we reached the sea shelf. With her behind my head, I couldn't see Alessa to judge her expressions or how she felt about treading into deep, open water.

"Come on. You scared?" Alessa teased. She threaded her fingers over the damp strands of dark hair below my fin. "Well?" As if sensing my concern, she devised the perfect system. "If I need air, I'll tug your mane, okay? Just a light tug. We'll pretend I'm freediving and you're my inflatable balloon to bring me to the surface."

When I remained reluctant, Hyrum bit my shoulder. I called him a few unpleasant names in our language, grateful Alessa couldn't hear our mental thoughts.

Helena chastised me, too. According to her, I should have had more faith in my chosen mate. Before the mare finished fussing at me, Zeno capitalized on the pause and charged ahead despite our plans for a race.

Cheater, I thought, spurred to action. I lurched forward and rushed after him with a big breath of air in my lungs. Alessa's strong thighs squeezed my ribs, a sign of her readiness. Taking her queue, I plunged beneath the surface and propelled forward through the cold water into the beautiful ocean. My home.

Of the four of us, Helena was the swiftest. We cut through a colorful school of fish and took Alessa on a merry chase through rock formations and vibrant coral growths. Each time she pulled on my mane we breached the surface for air then returned to our underwater exploration.

We played a variant of tag often reserved for foals and young hippocampi. With her on my back directing me, we hid and sometimes stealthily caught one of my herd mates unaware.

Her impressive breath control — years of training, diving practice, and a testament to her athleticism — astounded my friends while filling me with pride.

The final test came when we returned to shore and sprawled across the pale sand in our human bodies. They wanted to know more about her, and through me, asked multiple questions.

"Her skin is very pretty," Helena commented in our native tongue, touching Alessa's bikini-covered breast. My girl squeaked and slapped a hand over her own tit to shield it from further prodding. "Are all humans so colorful?"

"Dante, why did she poke my boob? What are you guys saying?"

I dropped my face into one palm and sighed. With no small amount of laughter, I described clothing and human modesty to my eager friends then in English, I explained their interest to Alessa.

"They think I'm funny because I'm wearing clothes?"

I nodded. "They've never seen swimsuits or clothes before up close, but you're welcome to take it off and join us if you want."

"Off?" she squeaked.

"My friends won't ogle you. Trust me."

I learned early on about Alessa's taste for exhibitionism when she allowed me to finger her on the porch our first night together. Testing her limits, I raised one hand to the back of her neck where the string secured her bikini in place. She didn't stop me. Her eyes remained on my face the entire time until the scrap of spandex fluttered to her lap.

While the men spectating her swim performance had leered with lust in their eyes, my fellow stallions gave only cursory glances.

Helena clapped with joy as Alessa helped her try on the bikini top. "Dante, can I have one of my own?" she asked, which I translated.

A warm, rose tint spread over Alessa's cheeks, the cool breeze tightening the pink peaks of each plump breast. "She's given me an idea. Dante? Invite them to come onto the island next time. We can show them so many things and introduce them to my world. Please? I want to pay them back for today."

Four curious faces studied me, waiting eagerly for the translation. Hyrum jumped at the opportunity, and before Zeno could decline, Helena accepted for both of them. He shot her a dirty look, sighed, and nodded his head.

"We will come. My mother will not be thrilled, but she will watch Dido while we are gone."

"Excellent. And what of you, Lycus?"

"Did you need to ask?" He grinned. "I would like to meet a fine human woman, too."

"Oh I cannot wait to return. She and I will have fun," Helena declared. She hugged Alessa close and pressed their cheeks together. "Dante, tell her I am very glad to know her."

"I think she's figured that out."

These two will become good friends, I decided.

Alessa painted a picture of the world beyond the sea. She told them of movies, restaurants, and evenings out with friends at dance clubs. In turn, Helena told her of our everyday life in and out of the ocean, our hobbies, and our Grecian island where we grazed in the Mediterranean sun. She even spoke of the berries our mares fermented back home.

"Dante was stinking drunk," Helena said. "He declared himself king of the sea and dragged himself into the water where he nearly drowned himself before Lycus saved him."

"I am not translating that."

"Coward."

We razzed one another a while longer until the sun kissed the horizon line. After my pals waded into the water, Alessa wasted no time in flinging her body against mine, pressing her stiff nipples to my chest.

I was hard as a rock in seconds, pulsing to full arousal.

"Yes," she half-whispered against my lips. Her tongue darted between them, questing for mine.

"Huh? Yes what?"

"Today was... absolutely beautiful, and I want to be your mate. I want you to claim me as your own."

It was the only encouragement I needed.

With her naked limbs molded against me, I drew her legs up around my waist, placing us in perfect alignment, and plunged into her tight grip.

The most heavenly sensation sheathed every inch. As I throbbed inside her, Alessa clung to my shoulders, her nails biting into my skin.

"Deeper, Dante. God this is amazing."

"I love the way you feel," I groaned out. My breaths turned shallow as I maintained the feverish rhythm she and my inner stallion preferred. Faster, more, deeper, she never hesitated to voice her needs to me.

Alessa leaned back, letting her arms fall away from my shoulders. Trusting me not to let her drown. I dipped forward and claimed one pink nipple between my teeth. Nibbling the sensitive peak made her core clench in a brilliant series of contractions. The taste of the salt water on them, her natural scent, and everything about her sensational body drove me crazy.

The buoyant ocean water made our position easy to maintain. I snuck a hand between our bodies and found her clit. Teased it. One flick was enough for Alessa to arch and moan my name.

I became wild with lust, surrendering to the animal inside me. My withdrawal provoked a startled cry of protest, but I ignored it to cradle Alessa in my arms. In five long steps through the water, I reached a jutting section of rock where I set her down facing away from me, her back to my chest.

"Hold on," I rumbled against her ear, a single warning for what was to come.

With her weight braced on the rock, its surface worn smooth from the waves, the feral beast in me took over and drove my aching cock straight into her with a single stroke before pulling back and thrusting into her again. Every time felt like the first, so tight she squeezed me almost to the point of pain. I groaned a guttural, low sound of pleasure and set my cheek against her shoulder.

Alessa's hips moved on a perpetual loop. Forward and back, she met the clash of my pelvis into her bared ass. With one arm around her waist to secure her against me, the other remained free to explore and squeeze one dimpled cheek.

The gentle waves crashed around us, rising as far as Alessa's waist at their highest. Sand shifted beneath our feet, the water dragging at us, but I held strong and firm.

"I'm yours Dante. All yours," she cried out in wild abandon. "Please, I'm so close."

"Mine," I agreed with her on a growl.

Nothing mattered but making her come again and again as she screamed my name. I wanted to lose myself in her body. My balls slapped against her upraised ass, a rhythmic thump of skin against skin each time our bodies joined.

She came on the next stroke. I fucked her through every contraction, riding her through toward a second climax because once wasn't enough for my filly.

When it came to her pleasure, I was insatiable. My stallion demanded more, urging me to bring her to the ultimate fulfillment. I had to drive out the memory of all other men who came before me until no one else mattered, no one existed, until her only sexual memory was of my cock plunging inside her.

"Dante," Alessa gasped. "I can't... I can't take... take anymore."

"You will," I moaned against her ear, nipping it with my teeth afterward. "Come for me again, baby." To guarantee it, my arm dropped from around her, slipping my hand between Alessa's thighs to find her swollen clit. One pass of my index finger over the small nerve bundle tensed her body from head to toe.

"Oh God, oh God...!"

As I strummed the sensitive pearl, Alessa's wet, tight heat squeezed my cock a second time and her knees buckled. Her orgasmic screams created a harmony with the crashing waves. She clutched the rock while her body quaked and trembled in my hold.

"Dante!"

I loved this woman so much it hurt. As she wailed my name, waves of euphoria swept through me and branded my soul. Mine. She was mine. And in claiming Alessa, I'd also given myself to her. The building tension finally burst, and in several hot pulses I emptied inside her.

Motionless, I savored the final moments in my mate's hot channel, treated to a series of delicious mini-spasms around my cock. I inhaled a deep breath, closed my eyes, and let my cheek rest against the back of her shoulder again. I didn't need to see her trembling legs to know they were useless beneath her. If not for me holding her up, she would have slipped beneath the water.

"Lessa?"

"M'fine," she slurred, drunk from passion.

Even if our child and I could only be in her life five or six months of the year, I would make each week count. I'd make every day a new adventure and do the best to fill her life with only joy.

I would, because she deserved nothing less.

Chapter 8

~ALESSA~

Explosive.

No other word expressed an inkling of what I experienced as he brought me to ecstasy. I held on to the rock as if it were a life ring on the open sea while Dante slammed into my body from behind. Heat flushed over my bare shoulders and my breasts bounced to the feverish rhythm set by his thrusts. My body felt as if it should be going up in flames, cooled only by the churning water around us.

"Come for me again, baby."

I couldn't. *I can't. It's too much, too much.*

Talented fingers slipped between our bodies. With a single flick of his index finger against my clit, Dante brought me straight back to a quivering state. Every muscle in my body pulled tight.

"Oh God, oh God…!"

My mouth opened in a soundless cry, the wind trapped in my lungs by the intensity surging through my core. Dante was an amazing lover, intuitive to the last stroke whether it was by his fingers or his dick.

I came and he followed, joining me in orgasm. Something indescribable seared me with raw emotion, a sensation only to be felt but not named. *Is this the bonding? Is this it?* It was like a flash fire consuming me with pleasure, a solar flare of ecstasy scalding me soul deep. I writhed between my new mate and the rock, tears streaming down my cheeks.

"Dante!" A harsh, guttural groan parted my lips, the sound unfamiliar as if it had come from anyone but me.

We stood together for what seemed like hours, the beating of my heart louder than the crashing of the ocean.

The slightest movement from him delivered a mini-orgasm. Post-climax contractions rippled throughout my core like tiny aftershocks. His cock never left the intimate embrace I offered, but we shuddered together until at last he was motionless behind me with his cheek against my shoulder.

"Lessa?"

"M'fine," I mumbled.

He chuckled and slipped out. "Sleep, love."

"But... I wanna..." Despite my protests, I surrendered to the exhaustion and allowed Dante to carry me. Hours later, my eyes opened to the sight of a starlit sky above us while a cool island breeze danced across my naked skin. I shivered and cuddled closer before taking in the familiar surroundings. I recognized the patio lounge chair beneath us.

"Are you okay?" His words ghosted over my ear.

"Mmm… where are we? Are we on Teo's veranda?"

"He and Marcy went to visit their friends in California. Said we can stay overnight and have full run of the house."

"Teo is an amazing friend," I mumbled. "And soul bonding is exhausting."

"It is," he said, chuckling. "For the human at least."

I envied him for having the energy I lacked. "You're like… a furry incubus," I mumbled into his neck. I twisted in his grip and slid my arm across his chest. The serene music of the outdoors coaxed me in and out of sleep, until at last I awakened to explore Teo's bungalow.

"Are we supposed to do the Adam and Eve thing the whole time? As much as I like seeing you naked, it's distracting."

Thankfully, Marcy had left clothes for me and Dante had finally broken down and planted his own wardrobe in the bungalow. Once our rumbling tummies motivated us to trek inside, we showered, raided the fridge, and found a dish clearly marked with our names. I squinted at him.

"Did you plan this?"

"Down to the last detail," Dante said, beaming with pride. "Did I do well?"

"Amazing."

I spent the time after our bonding wondering how I'd ever lived without it. It completed me, as if I'd been given more of myself, and even more of him. Days passed of me wondering if it was all a dream or psychosis I'd invented in my head — girl meets perfect boy, boy isn't human, boy cherishes her like a queen. I lived in a fairy tale and wondered when we'd have the first fight or grow tired of spending time together.

When it didn't come, I grew nervous and even skeptical.

"Why should I pick fights?" Dante finally asked as we stood at the dockside with our poles one evening after work. He'd invited me to go fishing with him. "I know you're accustomed to assholes, but I have nothing to gain from conflict with you." He kissed my forehead and held me close with one strong arm. I breathed him in, soothed by the perpetual scent of the beach I'd come to associate with him. "Nothing."

"Is this a you thing, or a hippocampus thing?"

"Both." He chuckled. "Hippocampi are pretty laid back unless we're in danger or pissed off. And I think we've skipped most of the common elements of relationship troubles."

"Well yeah. You kind of just moved into my place."

"We don't need to fight about money. You're welcome to what I have that Abuelo doesn't need."

"No thanks. I work for my own money."

"See."

"We're dull."

"We love each other," he said, flashing his best cocksure grin. I swatted his shoulder with one hand and baited my fishing hook again.

"Then teach me your language. I want to learn to speak with your people."

"It is a very old language. There are no computer tutorials for it.

"You can barely use a computer anyway. Come on. Teach me what you know."

Dante eyed me as if I were crazy, wanting to learn a supposedly dead language. "You're certain?"

"I'm serious. Maybe one day I can hold a conversation with your dad and prove I'm not an idiot human stealing you away."

"Fine. If you want to speak it so badly, you'll have to learn it the way I learned English and Spanish."

I then spent the remainder of the week fussing and swearing at a man who wouldn't speak English. He answered me in his native tongue for everything from "pass me the ketchup" at dinner to talking about his day. It was gibberish.

One day, instinct guided me to toss the remote into his lap in passing, automatic.

"How'd you know I wanted the remote?" He glanced up at me, bewildered.

"It was the only thing you could have been asking for."

When ancient words didn't exist for our modern conveniences, Dante created funny compounds that made me giggle. Control stick. Metal horses. Moving pictures. Eventually, some of the strange words began to stick.

Dante surprised me three weeks after our bonding by ushering four naked people into my house.

"What the hell?"

"You said you wanted them to visit us."

"I do, but give me some warning next time!"

I laughed despite the impromptu get-together, and within a few minutes, I'd wrung out and tamed Helena's massive amount of hair into a single plait. "She has a longer torso than me, but this sundress should fit her, I think. It'll do until we can get her into a resort shop."

"Good. She says she wants to wear pretty things to be beautiful like you," Dante replied.

"She's already gorgeous."

Helena beamed at me, as if she could understand my words.

I glanced out of my bedroom to see Dante's progress with the men. Hyrum, Lycus, Zeno, and Dante all wore swim trunks and reminded me of a boy band preparing to shoot a beachside music video. Next to Dante's sun-kissed brown, their skin tones ranged from lightly tanned to fair. I planned to liberally spray sunblock on Zeno who was like a milky ghost. I hadn't seen anyone so white since visiting an internet friend of mine in Wales.

Crap. I better spray her, too. They're so pale, I thought. Helena could have passed for an Irish woman.

With Helena dressed, we both stepped out from my bedroom. Zeno, despite his earlier reservations, grinned at his mate and smoothed his hands down the turquoise shirt Dante loaned him.

They looked happy enough to take a photo. So I did, ushering them outside onto my porch where the swaying palms provided the perfect backdrop. The sweltering summer sun heated my bare shoulders, exposed by the strapless maxi dress I'd chosen.

"Hey, I have a question."

Dante looked at me. "Yeah?"

"If Hyrum and Lycus are part of the guard, how did they get permission to come up to the surface?"

"Well…" Dante rubbed the back of his neck and grinned, sheepish. "Technically they snuck away and no one knows they're here."

"Is that safe?"

"The guard isn't necessary around here, despite what my father would have everyone believe. Kekoa's presence keeps the big predators away and we recognize him on sight."

I laughed. "I guess a tiger shark would be a good deterrent. Add in a dragon who likes to dive for fish and you have pretty safe waters."

Dante grinned. "Exactly. It's a perfect refuge for my kind."

"Yeah, sounds like it." My smile faded. I wished his people could stay forever, but the surrounding area could never sustain their large population year round.

And their herd's alpha, Dante's father, would never approve.

We took my new friends shopping first and gave them a mini tour of the island attractions. They pointed out things of interest and chattered excitedly about anything and everything from speeding dune buggies to the electric rail. We rode it for an hour to appease Zeno, who took a great fascination with its movement.

I had a great laugh at the silly expressions on their faces when we swung by the aquarium for the afternoon mermaid show. My friend Lana played the role of the princess in my stead, without as many underwater tricks or my breath control.

Afterward, we took them to the seaside grill and cafe, a place I loved for its sushi conveyor belt and happy hour. We introduced the guys to beer, which Helena and Hyrum loathed from the first sip. I hooked them with a taste of my margarita instead and crowed my victory over Dante when the mare declared that she loved it.

My pocketbook mourned my request for Dante to let me cover the costs of our outing, but I didn't regret a single penny spent. We ate like pigs and stuffed ourselves on slices of sashimi, garlic shrimp, and an assortment of other items the eager hippocampi requested to try.

"What do they think about their new clothes?" I asked before plucking the last piece of roe-dusted sushi from my small plate.

"Lycus isn't a fan, but Hyrum says he can get used to it." Dante grinned. "I didn't like it much at first either."

I glanced at him in his shorts and open shirt, the usual everyday style of my surfer boyfriend. "You clearly don't like it now either."

"I'm a surf instructor. Would you expect me to wear jeans? Speaking of surfing, the guys wanted lessons. I'm gonna go and grab my board. Watch them?"

"Of course I will. But really? Surfing?"

"I thought we'd try skimboarding instead. If Mrs. Courtland can do it, they can."

I grumbled.

We had plenty of beach for our fun and games. A crowd gathered to watch as we took turns running across the water covered sand and leaping on the board, skimming across like snowboarders.

Hyrum, Helena, and I took the most spills, while Zeno and Lycus appeared to be naturals on the board. After another tumble, Helena rattled off words in their native tongue. They were too quick for me to make anything out.

"What did she say to me?" I asked.

"She says she feels ridiculous," Dante answered me.

"I feel ridiculous, too. My ass hurts."

"You have enough of it to cushion the fall." One of his large palms copped a feel under the guise of soothing away my ouchies and dusting the sand from my skin. I wore one of my smallest swimsuits, a green bandeau top exposing my shoulders to the warm sun. The bottoms left just enough cheek exposed for him to grab. Until recently, I'd always felt shy about revealing skin on the beach and concealed my curves when away from the show tank during performances.

Sand clung against Helena's wet body from ankle to shoulder, fine golden grains against her itty black bikini. I helped her brush it off and sat on the sidelines with her while the guys behaved like children.

After the sun dipped below the horizon, the four hippocampi returned to the ocean under the cover of darkness. We promised to do it again soon.

"They seemed like they had fun." I hugged my body against my mate with one arm around him. My cheek found the perfect spot against his chest, listening to the pounding bass of his powerful heart.

Dante hugged me against his side and kissed my brow. "They did."

"So how come your dad is so against it?" The question had been bugging me ever since he told me about his father. "I mean, look at today. Nothing bad happened. They had a good time."

"It is a long story."

"So let's take a walk on the beach and you can share it with me."

Taking my hand in his, Dante led the way down the moonlit sand. For a time he was quiet and I didn't rush him. The cool water washed over our toes, swirling sand around our feet.

"My mother was murdered by someone. A diver shot her with a harpoon."

My heart stuttered, his words dampening my mood like a bucket of ice. "Do you remember it?"

"Vaguely… I remember… I remember it was my fault," Dante admitted. "I remember a man beneath the water with a bright spot light, and I was curious. I wanted to play with him because I'd met humans once while on this very island with my mother. I remember…" Dante's voice trailed and his dark brows furrowed. "Something pointing at me. My memory is foggy after that, but Dad found her with a harpoon spear in her heart."

I blinked my burning eyes a few times. No child should ever witness his mother's tragic death, but to make matters worse, Dante felt to blame for it. "That wasn't your fault, baby. You were a child doing what kids do best."

"I know. I don't hate myself anymore for it. Dad does enough of that for me."

"I'm sure he doesn't hate you."

"He won't even look at me most days, even if I talk to him. I've tried, Alessa. I swear on Triton's fin, I tried connecting with him, but if it isn't some matter concerning the herd, he won't hear me."

"What about your mother? Do you remember her much?"

"My mother loved this world," Dante admitted. "I can't hold what happened to her against all humans. I can't hate the world she introduced to me. Maybe I don't recall all our times together on the sand, but I remember the warmth of her love. I remember the feeling in here." He placed one hand over his heart.

"Is that why you came back as an adult?"

Dante nodded. "My father was against it but I swam ashore to look for Teo. He speaks our language and when I told him I wanted to meet the human who found me on the beach and took care of me, he arranged for a meeting with Abuelo. We hit it off, and the rest is as you know."

"Well, I'm glad you decided to come to land, even if your dad doesn't understand. Otherwise we'd never have met." I laced our fingers together and stood on tiptoe to kiss him. "So... I have work tomorrow, but I kinda used a favor up with a friend to get into that place you always eyeball when you think I'm not paying attention.

"I do not."

"You do, too, and I hope you're free because I want to take you out for a date-date."

"Is there a significant difference between a date and a date-date?" Dante asked.

"Mmhmm." I ran my fingers down his chest and followed the chiseled line between his abs until I traced his treasure trail. He responded to me in an instant, hardening noticeably beneath his shorts. "A date-date means I make extra effort to make your every wish come true. Every. Wish. No limits."

***

I dimmed the lights on our way out for the day, darkening the extravagant lobby to the aquatics center. With all of the junior staff gone for the day and our duties completed, the rest of us in supervisory positions were free to leave.

"I can't wait to see his face when we sit down. He's always doing things for me lately, and it's so nice to do something for him in return for once," I gushed as the three of us gravitated to the door.

Pam smiled at me. "You found a good one."

"Anyway. See you tomorrow, chica. Tell Dante we said hi," Julia said.

"Shit. I forgot my keys on my desk."

"Should we wait for you?" Julia asked. They lingered in the open doorway.

"Nah. I'm just gonna dart home to change anyway. Bye guys."

I sprinted back to my office and yanked the keys off the desk. On my way out, I encountered Doctor Castlebury. He held a clipboard in one hand. The other hung limply at his side, a casualty of a shark bite in his youth.

How does that man wear a turtleneck in this weather? Hasn't anyone told him he's on a tropical island? I wondered. Despite his ridiculous appearance, I forced a smile to my face and waved in passing. "Have a good evening, Victor."

"And where do you think you are going?"

I paused at the exit. He gazed at me with such earnest and questioning in his face, I wondered if something remained overlooked.

"Did you unload the shipment?"

"Shipment?"

"Was I not clear?" Doctor Castlebury aimed a thin smile at me. "We've received over five hundred kilograms of uncured live rock requiring your attention."

My hand dropped from the door knob. "From where?" My voice raised, cracking as I whirled to face him.

"We received a rather charitable contribution."

Castlebury approached to offer a clipboard displaying an inventory of our recent arrivals. My eyes nearly bulged when I read the rest. An aquarium on the mainland had gone out of business, sending several hundred pounds of rock and a few dozen delicate sea creatures to us.

"Bubble anemone? Lionfish?"

"Oh, yes. They arrived as well today. It was a rather large shipment of animals. Such a shame the aquarium is no longer in business."

"The time stamp on this list says you received it at noon, Victor. Noon!"

"It slipped my mind. Certainly you understand." His smile made him look like a shark. "At any rate, I expect this to be done prior to your exit from the complex this evening. Good day."

"This isn't fair! Victor, it's the end of the day. I can't do this."

"Leave it until morning then if it troubles you so deeply. The animals will simply remain in their shipment bags until your arrival."

My eyes skimmed the list and read the names of many exotic creatures, some hardy and others too delicate to be risked overnight. I swallowed and remained quiet, shaking with rage. He'd done this on purpose. He'd risked all of these animals to teach me a lesson.

A single telephone call to Teo would have fixed Castlebury — but I didn't want to abuse my friendship with the dragon. We typically reserved Teo for when a situation reached critical mass. Missing a date with Dante fell shy of reaching nuclear event status, but just slightly in this case. I had plans to sweep him away to a stupidly expensive reservation I'd never manage to pull off again at the most lavish seaside grill on Teo's island.

This is going to take hours. My eyes burned as I stared down at the intimidating list.

I worked hard and fast to initiate the time-consuming acclimation process for the most fragile new specimens. I was up to my elbows in saline water when Pam phoned me.

"Girl, where are you? I'm at your house with the shoes you wanted to borrow. Dante said you never came home."

"Shit! I forgot to…" I sighed. With less than two hours before our dinner date, my chances of completing my impossible set of tasks had vanished.

"Forgot to what?"

A minute later, I'd given Pam the rundown on everything, and broken down into tears.

"That fucker. Girl, we'll be right there. We'll just clock back in to help you."

I sniveled into the line and fumbled to tear a few Kleenex from a box on my desk. "I can't let you do that, Pammie. You guys are done for the d—"

"See you soon." The call ended.

Twenty minutes later when the doors opened, I hadn't stopped sobbing into my tissues. I was so pissed, so irrationally and impossibly angry that the tears wouldn't end.

"I told you guys, I can do this on my own."

The scent of the open sea surrounded me with a pair of strong arms. I peeked up into Dante's blue eyes. Pam and Julia stood behind him in the doorway, smiling at me.

"What are you doing here?"

"Pam told me what happened, so I came to help, too. I don't know anything about the scientific side of ocean life, but if you instruct me, I'll do it."

With direction, Dante wasn't a bad worker. I tried to offer him gloves for handling the live rock, but he waved them off and reached in with his bare hands. I chalked it up to male bravado until he whispered the secret to me: fish toxins and aquatic animal stings didn't pose a danger to hippocampi. It was part of their magic, in and out of human form.

I let the girls giggle over his badassery and carried on with the tedious water samples on the holding tank. All parameters appeared to be in order, saving me the time I would spend buffering with chemicals.

"Aren't your reservations at eight?" Julia whispered to me. "You have twenty-five minutes to spare."

"Yeah." I wasn't dressed for a romantic dine-in. I looked down at my damp shirt and frowned, unable to ignore the fishy scent on my clothes.

"Go. We'll finish up. Grab Dante and get out of here."

I shook my head. "I can't leave you guys here to fix Castlebury's mistake. He did this to punish me, *remember*?"

"Technically we're department supervisors and you're the assistant manager, which means we're your flunkies to boss at will," Pam reminded me.

"Whenever Castlebury pulls shit like this, we all have to own it. Not only you. Being his assistant doesn't make you his bitch," Julia said.

I snuck a glance at my man. He learned quickly, running another aeration hose into one of our barrels designated for uncured live rock.

"Why am I putting rocks into a barrel?" he asked suddenly. "I don't mind, but I'm curious."

"If we didn't take these steps, sediment and dying flora will pollute our marine environments."

We giggled at his blank stare, then Julia broke it down into something he could understand. By the time we finished, Dante and I were long overdue for our reservations, our table was gone, and I didn't feel sexy enough to pull off a last minute appeal for a spot in the restaurant.

So we went home instead. I soaked an hour in my clawfoot tub while Dante fetched dinner from Abuelo's. We feasted on fish and salsa verde then he painted my toenails neon green as I sprawled lifelessly on the sofa. I kept my feet on his lap when he finished.

Dante idly plucked grapes from a bowl with one hand, while the strong fingers of the other caressed my silky thigh, giving me shivers. At least my leg wax wasn't wasted. "Why do you look so glum, Alessa?"

"I wanted to have a romantic night with you," I admitted. "Now I'm too exhausted to even put my mouth on your cock."

"We *are* having a romantic night," Dante reminded me with an uncertain grin. "And you can always save your energy for the morning. I won't mind."

I leaned forward to swat him. "You're painfully good at painting toenails, but this was supposed to be a date out as a surprise for *you*. Instead, you're only doing something else nice for me."

"Eh," he said, shrugging his shoulders. "Making you happy makes me happy. Want some more grapes?"

"All I'm missing is a naked man with a feathered fan."

Dante chuckled and kissed my brow. "I can always ask Lycus to come up and assist. He's quite taken with you and upset you're without a sister."

"Nope. I'm good, but I do have a cousin. One hottie hippocampus is all I need."

And one hippocampus was the only one I wanted.

Chapter 9

~ALESSA~

Mom was due to reach the island on a lazy Sunday afternoon and according to last week's failed test, I still wasn't pregnant. I didn't know what to tell her about Dante yet, and I didn't plan to give her all of the gritty details. Around noon, I woke up with him beside me, struck by the urge to clean my small home from top to bottom. Again.

I opened all the windows to let in the fresh ocean breeze then tackled the bathroom and living room before my lover sought me out, naked as usual as I preferred.

"Should we be married?" Dante asked. His question came out of the blue, startling me as I scrubbed the stove to prepare for my mother's arrival and their inevitable introduction.

I arched a brow. "Why do you ask?"

"Because I want to know where your thoughts have gone. Normally when humans live together they're married, aren't they?"

"Not everyone." He eased his body behind me, more affectionate than lusty, and wrapped his arm around my middle. The pressure of his chest to my back warmed me.

"Does it mean something to you?" he asked.

"Well…" I bit my lower lip. "My parents weren't married when they had me, and that's okay. When I was a kid, I used to wish things were different. All of my friends had two parents and their dad's last name."

"Our family will probably seem strange. What will you tell people?"

It was a question I'd been asking myself for a while. "Honestly? I have no idea. Before we… bonded, I thought I'd tell them all we decided it wasn't working out and we were sharing custody." I smoothed my fingers over his dark waves, brushing errant strands from his face. "So maybe I'll tell everyone it's none of their damned business."

"Will your mother like me?"

"What's not to like?"

"Everything," he said with a grin.

Dante helped me tidy the rest of the house until the counters gleamed and the floors shined. The smell of citrus permeated my secondhand kitchen table, and he moved the sofa so I could vacuum beneath it.

If I didn't clean house thoroughly, my mother would do it during her vacation, and at my age I was too old for her to tidy behind me.

"Where will I sleep now?"

"At your own place with your grandfather," I teased.

Dante frowned. "I like sleeping beside you."

"And I love it when you sleep beside me." I kissed him then scurried away to pull on a pair of jean shorts beneath my t-shirt. "Okay, I'm gonna go down and pick her up. She and I have plans to eat at the hotel cafe for dinner so why don't you come by tomorrow for lunch."

"I have lessons booked all day. The group from Sweden."

"Oh yeah. They're coming to my afternoon performance. How about dinner after the show?"

"I'll be there."

Despite the big inconvenience of her decision to visit during the summer, my official time with Dante, I was glad to see Mom. I rushed into her arms and hugged her tight the moment I picked her out among the tourists disembarking from the ferry.

"You cut your hair!" Shock failed to sum up my feelings about her shoulder-length bob. Old photos of my mom revealed an incredible similarity in our appearances, as if I'd been taken and cloned directly from her. I had her red hair, my grandmother's red hair, and my great-grandmother's red hair — a family trait passed down each generation without fail.

"I wanted a change. Now, let me look at you." Mom held me out at arm's length. "You have such a lovely tan this year, but you're looking slimmer than you used to." Her lips pressed into a thin line. "Too slim."

"Mom," I groaned. "Believe me, I'm not starving myself."

"Are they working you too much?"

Between Castlebury's demands, the swim show, and my romping with Dante, time had become a valuable commodity. "No, nothing like that. I'm filling in for the mermaid program this season, is all," I fibbed.

"I thought you didn't do that anymore."

"One of the girls had a death in the family so she took an extended leave of absence. The owner of the resort personally asked me, begged me really, to take her slot."

"Oh, I'm sorry to hear that." My mom frowned at the news.

"Yeah, she's missed. So I've been getting extra exercise."

Mom sniffed. "Well, you're beautiful the way you are."

During the ferry ride to the resort we chatted about her recent promotion, gossiped over scandalous relatives, and eventually reached my house where Mom was eager to relax after a long flight. While she cozied on the couch, I fetched cold glasses of pineapple juice. When I turned, I saw her inspecting a bold, tropical print fabric beside her head. The kind of colors only Dante could pull off.

Shit! One of Dante's shirts, much too large for me to reasonably wear, hung over the back of the sofa in plain view of my mother. She plucked it up before I could hurry over to stuff it behind a loveseat pillow.

"This doesn't belong to you." Mom turned her gray eyes to me. "Do you have a boyfriend?"

Whelp. Cat's outta the bag now, I thought. "I do and you'll be meeting him at dinner tomorrow. He's busy with his grandfather this evening."

"You never said anything. Does that mean it's not serious or… it *is* serious?"

"You did just find his shirt. In my house. So…"

"Well, sit, spill it. What's the boy's name?"

"Dante."

Mom's eyes grew large. I giggled and tucked my chin, nodding. "Well. I'll finally get to meet this elusive Dante."

"Is that why you decided to pop up over during the summer this time?"

"Maybe," Mom said mysteriously. When she smiled, her eyes crinkled and faint laugh lines creased her freckled face. I wanted to age as gracefully as her. "You always talk about him. So is this a recent thing?"

"Yeah, it's a recent development. I think you'll like him though."

Despite Dante's concerns, no reason existed for why my mother wouldn't like him. I beamed proudly and showed her a photo of us together, taken only a week ago by Marcy.

"He's a handsome man," Mom murmured in approval. "But is he good to you?"

"The best. Doesn't let anyone disrespect me, cleans up after himself, and even cooks me breakfast in bed." I left out the naked part.

On our way to dinner, Mom grilled me about my boyfriend, how long he'd been living with me, if he planned to remain a surf instructor all of his life, and whether or not I would ever move home. I power walked to the hostess and informed her of our reservation, abruptly ending the game of twenty questions.

Mom resumed it at the table.

"He looked Italian in your photograph. Is he Italian?"

"Yes and no..."

"Have you met his parents?" she asked, as the waitress arrived with the wine.

"His dad's a difficult guy. They don't get along, and his mom was murdered when he was a child."

"Oh." Mom frowned. "I'm sorry to hear that."

I raised my wine for a sip, needing it to make it through Mom's questioning.

"Are you being safe?"

Wine went down the wrong hole, choking me. "Mom!" I sputtered. Coughing into a napkin with tears in my eyes, I struggled to clear my airway. "What kind of question is that?"

"A good one," she replied, appearing very stern.

Technically, we were practicing safe sex. We were a mated, monogamous couple, the very equivalent of marriage in the paranormal community. And while making a baby was a normal, acceptable activity for married couples, I became reluctant to express our intentions to my mother. I directed the conversation to another topic instead. "Mom, did you really come all of this way to quiz me like we're on Jeopardy?"

"Well, no... I'm sorry. I rarely see you, you never visit home, and I never know what's going on in your life anymore."

Leaving sex with my boyfriend behind, I told mom about my work at the aquatics department, my recovered sea turtle Kai, and I promised to show her photos I took while snorkeling off the owner's personal island.

"I love snorkeling," she sighed. "How is the view here?"

"Magnificent. If I ask Teo, I'm sure he'll let me and Dante bring you back." A smile tugged the corners of my lips. "Didn't you tell me how much you wanted to learn to skimboard one day? He's amazing at it."

Mom pursed her lips thoughtfully. I didn't need to read her mind to know she thought time learning to skimboard was a chance to examine my man.

Later, after dinner, the two of us settled on the sofa together beneath a blanket to watch a movie. The long flight had exhausted her, and my hectic schedule wore me thin. My mother's hugs were the best comfort after a hellish week. When her head drooped, I sent her off to my bed and remained on the sofa.

I awakened in the morning to the smell of fresh bread in the oven. Mom always arrived with expectations of feeding me well, so I kept a mix of fresh ingredients and frozen dough.

"Okay, I have a day planner and a resort schedule right here for you. I can't stay long, because I told my department manager I'd be there to oversee cleaning the tanks today and then we have a show this afternoon."

"They *are* working you too much," she accused.

"Well…" I poured myself a cup of milk while my mother sipped her coffee. "It's getting me out of student loan debt and it's only for a summer."

"You should have attended college at home."

"I wanted to spend the time with Daddy, you know that."

Mom's expression softened. "You are right. Pay me no mind, Alessa. I worry about you missing the best years of your adulthood."

Like you once did? I wondered. *Did my existence lead you to feel robbed of a full life?*

"Mom, I live rent-free on a resort. I swim with dolphins. My boss pays me to play with turtles."

"All right. All right. You have a dream job, I only wish it was closer to home is all."

"I'll come home during the winter break, Mom, I promise."

"I'll hold you to it."

I chugged my milk and scurried into the bedroom to collect clothes for the day. In passing, I kissed the top of her head. "I am fine, so don't worry about me."

She may have believed me if I didn't puke promptly after stepping out of the shower. Most of it hit the toilet bowl.

"Baby, are you okay?"

"I'm fine, Mom. I think the milk went bad. Dante doesn't drink it and it takes forever for me to use up a gallon."

I washed the sour taste from my mouth and emerged. Mom wasted no time; she touched my brow and felt my lymph nodes, reminding me of when I was a child claiming to be too ill for school.

"You don't feel warm. Does it hurt anywhere?"

"It was probably something I ate last night." I smiled wearily.

My mother remained unconvinced by my thread-thin excuse. "I ate the exact same thing as you and I'm fine."

"Just a bug then, Mom." The flimsy explanation fell through when I bolted for the toilet again.

"Alessa, honey, have you had your period this month?"

"Er…"

"Maybe you should take a pregnancy test."

"Mom!"

"Look, sweetie, I'm not judging. I'm just pointing out a possibility. Do you want me to run up to the store and grab you one?"

"No, that's all right. I have a box."

My mother arched a brow but didn't say anything. A lie came to mind, but I kept my mouth shut. I hated fibbing to her. Once I'd shut her out of the bathroom, I endured the longest sixty second wait of my life. To be dramatic, I prayed to every god I could recall by name, from the god of Christianity to Zeus and the sea god Poseidon. I tried not to leave anyone out, an equal-opportunity wish maker.

Finally, I opened my eyes and peeked at the stick. Two pink lines, a clear pregnancy result, darkened across the tiny white window. Where had that been last week when I tested twice?

"Well?" Mom demanded.

I sagged against the bathroom sink and exhaled a deep, relieved sigh. Tears stung my eyes within moments and trickled down my cheeks. We'd made it in time, with months to spare. Time enough to prove to his father our mating could be successful after all. Time enough to save Dante from the rear guard.

My mother knocked again and threatened to pick the lock, so I saved her the trouble and opened the door. Without a word, I showed her the positive test then set it down.

"Oh, honey…" Happiness warred with concern on her freckled face. "Are you okay with this?"

"I am, Mom. I really am. I wanted to save this for after you met Dante but… I love him and we're getting married. I mean, we talked about it."

She squealed and threw her arms around me. We hugged and bounced in place together for a few seconds before she finally let me go.

"You have to go tell him," Mom said. "Can you call in sick?"

"I have to check on a few things but I'll take off early and— crap. Dante has a tour group booked today. Do you think you can keep the news between us so I can tell him after dinner?"

"I can do that," she confirmed. "Besides, it'll give me a chance to size my future son-in-law up."

Eyeing my mother up and down, I sighed. "He's worried you'll hate him, so please take it easy. Try not to scare him away."

"When have I ever scared any of your boyfriends?" Mom scoffed.

"Alexi Papadopoulos comes to mind."

"Yes, well…"

I kissed her cheek and grinned. "He was a loser anyway. You go have fun and I'll pick you up here for dinner at six."

Everything about today was going to be great. I laced my hands over my belly and dreamed of the life growing within. Would it be a little boy with his father's bright smile or a girl with my stormy gray eyes?

As tempting as it was to tell Pam and Julia, my pregnancy remained a secret to share with Dante alone. I floated throughout the work day from one task to the next and even smiled in the face of Castlebury's attitude.

"Something's gone wrong with my printer."

"Can't you have David fix it?"

"David is unavailable. You, however, are standing about."

I glanced at the laundry list of tasks on my desk, from equipment orders to time clock corrections for the floor staff. *I'm going to kill this bastard with kindness.* "Sure. I'll be in to fix your printer in a second."

"Excellent."

"Douche," I muttered after he left. The man was always jamming up his printer, but he couldn't be bothered to learn how to open the machine and fix it on his own. It wasn't even a difficult repair.

I handled several reports then headed over to Castlebury's office. His voice reached me through the door, causing me to slow and linger. A peek through the cracked opening revealed the man at his desk, phone to his ear.

"I have a fully equipped boat ready to head out on the water," Castlebury said into the phone. "Yes, yes. Of course. Acquire the specialty gear as discussed and we shall be good to go. No. No. Multiple harpoons will be necessary."

What the heck is he planning? Probably something that'll wind up making me pull ridiculous hours. The last time Victor went out on his boat he came back with wild specimens that didn't adapt well to confinement and (inspired) Teo's rule about acquiring our animals through channels authorized by him only.

"You'll be handsomely paid for your time, I assure you. When we're done, we'll both be rich men…" His eyes raised to me from the computer screen as he hung the phone up. "Something I can help you with, Miss Kokinos?"

"Your printer, Victor. You asked me to come fix your printer."

I did it hastily, hoping to be in and out before he could initiate small talk.

"Employee productivity has taken a dramatic decline this summer," Castlebury murmured from his desk chair. "What do you plan to do about it?"

"Maybe an employee appreciation luncheon? Reward the ones who perform up to standards to inspire everyone else?"

Doctor Castlebury's brows raised. "Excellent idea, Miss Kokinos. Perhaps during the week while most staff members are available? Wednesday would be suitable."

"Really?" My mouth dropped, but I quickly recovered. "Oh, yes. Yes. Definitely. I'll get on arranging that. Um... my mom is in town, so I wondered if I can take off early and have the rest of the week with her. I'll come in Wednesday for the party."

Victor dismissed me with a hand wave then faced the computer. The printer beeped and clicked, creating electronic sounds as it cranked out sheets of printed text. "As much time as you need."

"Thank you, Victor."

Before the alien wearing my boss' skin could emerge and eat me, I scurried from the room and tracked down Pam in the employee lounge.

"Castlebury is being nice today," I whispered. "Any idea what's up?"

"No idea. His usual fishing trip, I think. He scheduled off a week soon."

"I think he's treasure hunting or something. He was talking to someone on the phone about boats, gear, harpoons, and getting rich. Thankfully he's not Nick Cage, so we don't have anything to worry about here."

Pam snorted. "Well, good luck to him then. Maybe if he finds gold he'll quit."

After we shared a laugh at Castlebury's expense, I typed up a quick flyer about the party and posted copies to our employee bulletin boards.

Mom caught the afternoon performance in the tank. I spotted her through the glass and waggled my fingers in her direction. She gave a thumbs up for my new tail and snapped photo after photo. As much as I lived for mystifying the audience, I couldn't wait for the damned summer to end.

I puked in the trash can in the women's changing room when I caught a whiff of someone reheating fried chicken in the microwave. The girls fussed over me but accepted my food poisoning excuse. I cleaned myself up and met Mom outside by the fish tanks.

"Ready for dinner? I got us a table at the Mediterranean restaurant."

"Ooh, I loved that place last time I flew over. Still, I'm more interested in your young man."

"Mom," I whined.

"Don't worry," she said. "I'm just excited to meet him, is all." Her attention drifted to a middle-aged man studying the adjacent tank. I admired the muscular blond with her in passing, then we strolled arm-in-arm down the flora-lined paths through the resort grounds. I pointed out my favorite shops, some of the resident animals, and chatted about Dante.

"So what about his family? Do they live on the island, too?"

"His grandfather runs a little hut on the beach with the best fresh fish."

"We'll have to try it out while I'm here."

At the restaurant, I gave my name to the hostess and she said Dante was already waiting for us. She led the way inside the air conditioned building to a table toward the back beside the windows overlooking the ocean. At our approach, Dante rose to his feet.

Five years of friendship had taught me Dante's wardrobe only consisted of shorts and obnoxiously bright shirts, but the sight of him in a suit stole my breath away. The perfect cut had been tailored to his broad shoulders with an inseam suitable to his impressive height, and he wore Italian leather shoes to round out the immaculate charcoal-colored suit. My eyes darted to the silk tie beneath his pristine, starched white collar. The blue matched his eyes, overlaid with a white diamond pattern grid.

I'd recognize Teo's trinity knot anywhere. He'd worked his billionaire dragon magic and transformed my humble surfer into an elegant gentleman. Somehow, I managed to blink away the tears springing to my eyes.

"Mom, this is Dante. Dante, my mom." I wiped my sweaty hands against my skirt a few times, petrified. I snuck a glance at her, only to find my fears were unjustified. Mom's mouth opened and closed wordlessly.

"It is my pleasure to meet you, Ms. Kokinos. I have waited a long time for this day." Dante bowed courteously then offered his hand.

Won over by either his good looks or impeccable display of manners, Mom pushed his hand aside and hugged him. "Please, call me Pelagia. My daughter informed me about the marriage plans in the making, which means you'll be family soon." Mom glanced over her shoulder and winked at me.

Way to be subtle, Mom.

"Yes, there are plans." He squeezed her back, relief evident on his face. Once Mom stepped back, she gazed over him again and nodded her head in approval. "I've made arrangements for a small ceremony this week."

He what?!

"Good." My mother smiled, oblivious to my wide-eyed confusion behind her.

We took our seats and ordered our drinks; water for me and wine for Dante and my mom. I figured I could have a sip or two from his glass. The moment my mother excused herself to the women's room, I kicked Dante beneath the table. "Plans for a ceremony? Since when?"

"Since today," he answered. His grin reappeared, the one I'd come to love — one part arrogance to two parts adorable. "You were away when I went to pick up my suit from Teo, so I didn't have the opportunity to discuss it with you." He didn't apologize for the snap decision, and frankly, I didn't want him to. The sudden take-charge attitude turned me on as much as it thrilled me.

Dante put on a flawless performance as my handsome fiancé. I beamed proudly beside him and held his hand throughout dinner. It turned out that I couldn't tolerate the smell of beef any more than I could fried chicken. Dante and I stuck to the elaborate salad bar. I took generous portions of grilled shrimp, marinated artichoke hearts, and seaweed salad while my mom sampled their Greek offerings off the menu. For dessert we ordered fresh made baklava and almond cookies served with coffee, then followed our meal with a lazy, scenic stroll back to my home.

"It's been a true pleasure to meet you, Dante." Mom hugged us both when we reached my doorstep then stepped inside to grant us privacy.

"Will you walk with me for a few?" I asked him.

"Sure."

He waited until we rounded the corner on the stone walking path before a thousand questions came from him. "Do you really think she likes me?"

"My mom loved you. Trust me, she wouldn't have had a word to say to you if she disapproved."

With our fingers interlaced, we made our way down toward the beach. The stone path was lit by a pair of hanging solar lanterns every fifteen yards. I moved aside for a broad-shouldered blond man to pass us. He looked as if he'd been chiseled from marble. Something about him struck me as familiar.

"Did you mean it about wanting to be married, Dante?"

"Of course I meant it. If marriage is the human way, why shouldn't I want to make you happy?"

"But will it make you happy?" I asked uncertainly.

Dante's warm laughter snaked around my heart, granting me the perfect amount of encouragement. "*You* make me happy." He turned to face me on the narrow trail and set both hands on my hips, treating me to the hard outline of his body and perfect muscles I knew by memory.

A few tourists passed by and veered out of our way, taking the sandy route away from the light and our romantic moment. I ignored them all in favor of gazing into his blue eyes. At some point during the course of our friendship I'd become impossibly, hopelessly in love with my best friend. And I'd have it no other way.

"Come on. This way," I whispered to him. Our fingers laced, my hand a perfect fit against his palm. We moved onto the beach, and once we were alone again, I captured him by a handful of his dark hair, dragging him down to kiss me. "We did it."

"Did what?"

I giggled against his lips and whispered, "I'm pregnant."

At first, he stared, as if he didn't understand the words coming from my mouth. His stunned silence ended with a whoop and then he swept me into his arms, spinning me around on the moonlit beach.

In that moment, nothing but the two of us mattered.

"Really?" he asked, refusing to set me down. The tips of my toes skimmed the damp sand.

"Positive. I took a test this morning." *After throwing up everywhere... He doesn't need to know about that. Not tonight, anyway.*

Dante ran his fingers through my hair, smoothing my bangs away from my face. His kisses never got old, each one setting my soul on fire with the same intensity as the last. "I promise you I will be the best father for our child."

"I know you will."

Chapter 10

~DANTE~

We decided to wait a couple days before spreading the news to my herd. I kissed Alessa one more time for luck, handed her my trunks, then waded into the water until it lapped against my thighs.

"Good luck!" she called.

I glanced over my shoulder at her and grinned. "Two hours tops."

"I'll be here."

In daylight hours, our herd grazed amidst the ocean plant life between rounds of playful frolicking.

A colt fell beside me, adopting my stroke rhythm to keep pace.

"Hello, Taavi."

"Will you play with us today?" the youngster asked.

My path to Dad took a delayed detour until we'd had three rounds of tag and the little ones were satisfied. One day, in the not-so-distant future, my foal would be among their number.

"Good day, Delia," I called through our link, spotting the ivory-furred mare my father had taken for his new mate. She jerked her head up, startled by my enthusiastic greeting.

"Hello, Dante," she greeted me uncertainly.

"Is my father near?"

"Above us."

I bowed my head to her and swam up to our cavern's rocky surface. Dad frequently monitored the amount of grass and tropical life available to sustain our numbers. It was part of his job as our alpha, the boss who made sure we remained safe and fed. I'd watched him take on a shark once alone without the rear guard to have his back.

I could never be my dad. Or could I? For Alessa or our child, I'd take on a swarm of them.

"Father?"

"You've returned."

"I have news to share."

Adon moved toward me across the wet sand, swift despite his muscled bulk. "Yes, I am well aware."

"What?" *He knows? But how? We've told no one except her mother.*

"Did you believe such behavior would slip beneath my notice? That I would not realize two members of my guard have gone not once, but twice to the surface?"

"Father—"

"Perhaps you think me to be stupid or too blinded by my trust in you to realize what you have done."

"I never meant to displace your trust in me. I only wanted to show them there was a world above us full of people who are kind, and interesting things to learn. That's it. Nothing more."

I couldn't breathe. Nothing about this had gone the way I imagined it in my head. I had hoped he would for once, for once since my childhood, embrace me as his son again. That he would love me and take pride in my actions.

My head drooped further, my muzzle pointing toward the mossy rock beneath my webbed hooves. *This will never change. It's now or never, I have to stand up to him for once in my life.* "I took them because we are not your slaves, or your servants. You speak of the Phoenician people enslaving us as their animals then behave as if we are owned by *you.* What need do you have for Hyrum and Lycus here? If you punish anyone for what's occurred, then punish me, Father. *Me.* I acted against your orders and convinced the others to come to the surface."

Adon stiffened, a mountain of golden-furred muscle before me. "What did you hope to accomplish?"

"To show them there is more to life than the sea. To help them understand the world above. You think me foolish, but all I have ever wanted was to share my life with you, Father. To prove I'm not the waste you think I am."

"Well. You have succeeded. I have never felt more pride for you as my son as I do now."

I prepared myself for the worst, expecting a violent tongue lashing. When it didn't come, I stared as if he'd grown a second tail. "Proud?" I repeated.

Adon's shape shifted and shrank. The memory of my father's human form didn't match the man standing before me. I stared at him, too stunned initially to speak as I took in the shoulder-length blond hair and muscles as impressive as mine.

"You were there. I saw you. I saw you at the beach, but I — I didn't recognize you." Like my father, I took my human shape and stared at him in awe.

"I wished to see your filly with my own eyes. I wanted to understand your fascination and the justification for this defiance. She is radiant, my son, but more importantly, she made you smile."

"Of course she makes me smile, Father. I love her."

"I have not watched you smile since you were a boy." My father inhaled a breath and squared his shoulders. "Since your mother's passing."

I could speak the same of him. "You came up to spy on us?"

"As I said. I wished to see her with my own eyes. When I ventured onto land, I sought the resident dragon of the island as I once did years ago to find you. He spoke well of her, enough to pique my interest. She swims like a fish, graceful in the water even with that false tail."

"You watched her show?"

"I did. She carries nereid blood in her veins, I am certain. Something about her reminds me of the old stories from when the water nymphs frolicked with the humans, as we once did."

His words stunned me, but they made sense. *Is this why we're so drawn to one another? Because she has sea nymph in her bloodline?*

If such was the case, our child would be twice blessed.

"Now, what am I to do about your escapades with Hyrum and Lycus? Their place is here, protecting the herd. Not gallivanting about in the human world."

"I have a thought about that, father."

Adon arched a brow. We returned to our hippocampus shapes to achieve a measure of comfort we sometimes lacked as humans. "Speak," he voiced in our natural communication.

"Allow members of the guard to voluntarily join, Father. The days of old are long past. Let us be the ones to decide. Allow fathers to protect their foals and sacrifice if they choose. Don't bar them."

"But the mares—"

"Will understand. For once, I believe the humans have the right idea. Their men take pride in becoming warriors to defend their homes. There, it is an honor, not a position of shame to fear. They wish to protect their loved ones. Their people."

"Unbelievable."

"Their mares fight as well."

His eyes widened in disbelief. "Their women fight?"

"Voluntarily. They eagerly commit to fight alongside males sworn to the service."

A rare, quiet chuckle came from the stallion who never smiled. "One change at a time, Dante. You know as well as I do that great change takes time to implement with our people. We are stubborn. Perhaps someday our mares will fight, but for now I will consider your other suggestion."

Yes. One change at a time. I nodded in an effort to control the tight feeling in my throat, emotion burning my eyes with an upsurging of joy. "Thank you, Father. Thank you. Now I have news to share with you."

"More news? You are full of words today. I suppose the fault, however, is mine. I have given you little chance to speak freely of your thoughts."

It was the closest to an apology I had ever received. "I hope these words will please you."

"Then share them."

"I came to tell you Alessa carries my child."

"I am to become a grandfather?"

"You are."

Dad caught me off guard with the ferocity of his affection. My father hadn't embraced me since the day Teo reunited us on the shore, always keeping me at arm's length. In one hug, I knew he'd never stopped loving me, and while I could never understand the reason for his distance, I chose to forgive.

Leaning against him, I rested my face on his golden neck. I exhaled a relieved sigh and closed my eyes, soaking in the warmth.

~ALESSA~

I stood alongside the water with my arms crossed against my chest, Dante's trunks balled in one fist. "What took you so long?" I demanded when he returned. He answered by shaking water from his body, splattering me with errant drops.

"No, no!" I cried with both of my hands out in front of me. His shorts were a poor shield from the water, and my open palms failed to ward off his attention. Dante bumped his muzzle against my chest and soaked my shirt.

"You ass. I just got cleaned up for the staff party!"

He shrank down to his human form. "Sorry… not sorry."

I resisted the urge to slap the cocky look off his face. "Anyway, are you going to come with me? Mom is getting a body massage and mineral soak at the spa."

The party was in full swing when we arrived. I brought my donation, a tray of stuffed crabs and my mother's homemade tulumba. Each bite of gooey pastry tasted like deep-fried heaven and guaranteed they'd go quickly.

"There you are!" Pam almost bowled me over with her enthusiastic hug. "This turned out great."

"Hey, where's Julia? I have something to tell you both."

Once we located Julia, I delighted in sharing my pregnancy news with my two best friends. We squealed, hugged, hopped up and down, and then the gossip spread amongst our coworkers. A couple guys patted Dante on the shoulder in congratulations, but the reveal shocked no one.

Dante and I had truly been the last to realize we were in love.

"Okay, okay! I have gift cards!" I announced. "While all of you are terrific employees, Doctor Castlebury and I chose the most exceptional to award for your hard work and diligence."

I passed out fancy gift baskets, certificates to shops, and notified key employees of raises.

"Hey Alessa, snap my photo with my certificate?" one of the men called over. "My kids'll get a kick out of it if you can do it by the shark tank."

"Sure."

Crap, I forgot to swap memory cards, I noticed when I powered it on again and saw the depleted space. My camera had gone neglected since the swim with Dante's herd mates.

I shrugged it off and stepped onto the floor to take photos of mingling staff members. Castlebury arrived well into the luncheon. His khaki slacks and white button-up shirt was the most casual I'd seen the man who favored slacks and ties.

Once photos of all the awardees and raffle winners filled my camera, I returned to my office and plugged into the desktop. Hundreds of digital images spread across the screen in thumbnail size until I enlarged the icons for a closer look.

Smiling fondly, I swept through winter photographs of New York City with Daddy. I wished he was alive to meet Dante, but most of all, I regretted he wouldn't be around to meet his grandchild.

Switching folders, I pulled up the most recent pictures and selected a few without goofy expressions or closed eyes. Another sporadic wave of nausea hit me after I chose the print option on the day's photos. I abandoned the computer and hurried into the restroom.

"Morning sickness?" someone asked.

"You know it." I washed my face with cold water. "Except, you know, at all hours and not just in the morning."

The older woman chuckled and patted my back in sympathy. She suggested I keep saltines in my purse, a tip I wisely filed away. I wasn't about to turn away suggestions from those who had already been through pregnancy and childbirth.

Returning to my office, I found Castlebury sitting behind my desk, clicking through my computer. I couldn't see the screen, but panic immediately clawed at my heart.

"Can I help you, Doctor?"

"Ah, Alessa, there you are. Julia told me you'd taken photos prior to my arrival."

"I'm printing them out now but had to make a bathroom run."

"Yes, I heard congratulations are in order."

"Um, thanks. Look, not to be rude or anything, but I have personal photos on there, if you don't mind. I can send you everything from the party tomorrow," I offered.

"My apologies." Castlebury wore a contrite expression, but his eyes seemed too bright. The man never, ever apologized for anything. He hopped up from my chair and strode from the office without a backward glance.

I hurried around my desk and plopped down, searching my screen for any sign of what he'd been looking at. The printer continued chugging photographs out on the expensive glossy paper and the only picture folder open was the party. I breathed a sigh of relief then noticed a minimized tab.

Why is my email open? I wondered. When I bent over the computer, I saw a tiny 'email sent' notification in the corner. I hadn't sent an email.

I investigated the sent folder and found a recent letter to V.Castlebury. My blood ran cold, chilling my entire body from head to toe. I downloaded the attachments in the email and opened them, revealing five precious photos of Dante's herd mates and my underwater exploration.

"No, no, no," I pleaded.

I rushed out onto the employee floor to search for Castlebury, but he was nowhere to be found. He'd made his discovery and hightailed it to parts unknown.

Because of me, another human had been made aware of the hippocampi.

***

Telling Dante about my failure was the hardest and it cast a dismal shadow over an otherwise cheerful event. I'd let him and his herd down, endangering the very people who would one day protect my daughter.

Dante decided to keep the news from his father, fearing it would strike a critical blow to their newly rekindled relationship. Instead, seeking advice, we found Teo that same evening and told him.

"Bah," Teo said. He offered me a mug of tea. "You worry over nothing."

"He has photos of them, Teo. Real photos of five hippocampi. What if they're what he's been out there looking for all this time on his exploration dives?"

"Are you not jumping to conclusions, Alessa? You worry over nothing but a few insignificant photographs."

"You know as well as I do that he's always rambling about some sea monster he met in his youth. What if this is it and he's been looking for proof all this time?"

Teo rubbed his chin thoughtfully. "It would explain why a doctor of his background would come to this resort. He could work anywhere in the world."

"See!"

The dragon chuckled. "Relax, Alessa. I promise to you that within the next two weeks, all shall be fine."

As Thursday and Friday crawled by, my fear worsened and I dreaded the outcome. Dante didn't blame me, but I had difficulty sleeping at night and feared any day, I'd turn on the television to a news report announcing the scientific discovery of a new species. I glued myself to my computer during the days, keeping an eye on marine biology outlets, online journals, and even Facebook groups like I Fucking Love Science.

No one reported it.

My mate urged me to focus on our wedding instead, so my mother dragged me out to the mainland to purchase the perfect dress. She chalked my nervous behavior up to the pregnancy and impending matrimony.

Saturday morning dawned bright and beautiful without a single cloud in the sky to threaten our beachside wedding ceremony. It was small and intimate, with only a handful of close friends, my mother, Dante's grandfather, and Teo's family. Next to the discovery of my pregnancy, it quickly became the happiest day of my life. I stood beside the man I loved, hand-in-hand with him while wearing a cream sundress in lieu of white. The shell and pearl necklace he'd made for me graced my neck, a breathtaking replacement for a traditional wedding ring. The smile never faded from Dante's lips, and at the end, our first married kiss tasted as sweet as the day he first took me in his arms at the cabana.

Following the ceremony, I spied a single equine shape amidst the waves. The sun glinted against unmistakable golden hair, and from Dante's description of his father I knew it had to be him. I whispered in my new husband's ear and together, we stole a glance at the distant hippocampus.

I'd never forgive myself if Castlebury used my photographs to harm them.

I wouldn't lose this creature's trust. I couldn't.

***

"I thought humans had specific traditions to follow after a marriage." Dante's warm breath played over my ear as he teased me.

"You mean like the wedding night and honeymoon?"

"That, and…" He scooped me up in his arms outside the door to the suite. "Teo told me it's customary to carry the bride inside."

With his hands occupied, I swiped the keycard and pushed the door opened. Vases full of creamy white, pink, and yellow plumeria lined the entry hall and red rose petals scattered across the floor. The floral trail led to a table sprinkled with more petals laid out around a silver tray covered in strawberries and chocolate truffles. A matching ice bucket held a bottle of sparkling cider.

"It's beautiful," I whispered. I'd have to thank Teo and Marcy for the gift.

"Not as beautiful as you."

We shared a lingering kiss, the sort we couldn't have with our friends and family watching. Our wedding kiss had been short but sweet.

"I'm going to go freshen up," I said after we came up for air. His kiss alone dampened my panties and left my head buzzing.

"As you like. I will open the bottle."

I giggled as he set me down, picturing a geyser of bubbly cider all over him and the room. "Do you know how?"

Dante rolled his eyes. "I received a little instruction before tonight. Give me some credit."

Teo, I guessed. *I owe him a thank you card and… what the hell do you gift a dragon?* "I'll be out in a few, okay?"

I left Dante behind to marvel over the extravagant suite and room service menu. When Teo told me our gift included a two night stay, I filled our luggage bag with a world of possibilities. I'd even brought the vibrator I'd shyly hidden from him at home, tucked in the bottom of my panty drawer.

About a week ago when I first mentioned our wedding plans to Pam and Julia over the phone, they'd surprised me by adding to my lingerie wardrobe. According to them, there wasn't enough time to throw together an official bachelorette party, and Dante was hot enough to make any stripper appear inferior.

I glanced at my choices, biting my bottom lip as I tried to decide which I liked best for this night. On one hand, I had pristine white silk, virginal and sheer. On the other, I had a sexy one-piece number woven from black lace. The crotchless ensemble had made me blush when Julia suggested it. It reminded me of Dante, the perfect reason to select midnight fabric over the traditional shade of purity.

After donning the skimpy negligee, I checked out my reflection in the mirror. From the front, it appeared to cover as much as a bathing suit, but a thong exposed both of my cheeks in back.

I hope he's into lingerie. This thing isn't remotely comfortable.

I tossed the matching black robe onto my body and belted it before emerging.

Dante awaited me when I stepped through the door, sprawled across our honeymoon bed without a stitch of clothing. As usual, he took my breath away, but I couldn't tell if he'd stripped to get comfortable or in expectation of our night together. Both ideas made me giggle. One look allowed me to determine it was the latter.

"What?"

"Well, aren't *you* ready."

His tall cock stood at attention, the perfect invitation for me to climb astride him. I resisted and approached him with my sexiest, most seductive walk. I stopped at the bedside and held my pose. My husband rippled with muscle from his broad shoulders to his taut abs, a sight so perfect my core ached in anticipation.

"Gonna unwrap me?"

My new husband didn't need a second proposition. Crawling across the sheets, he reached out with one hand and tugged my belt loose, parting the lacy fabric. With a single nudge, the robe slid back from my shoulders and fell to the floor, exposing the form-fitting lace stretched over my body. Dante sucked in his breath, his cock twitched, and I beamed with satisfaction.

"How do you like it?"

"The wrapper or the gift? You could have worn a piece of tin foil and I'd be excited."

"You haven't seen the best feature." I joined him on the bed, on my knees with my legs apart, then placed his hand between my thighs.

"Humans make the most amazing things," he said. His fingers dipped into my wet slit and two penetrated my depths. I rocked my hips to his rhythm, inviting him to plunge deeper and faster.

I cupped both hands to Dante's cheeks and kissed him without restraint, releasing the raw passion pent up during our wedding.

"Lay back," I whispered against his lips. "I have a special treat for you."

He obeyed without question, always eager to please me in some way.

I shifted my body around until I knelt over him. With my knees framing his head, I straddled Dante's face and leaned forward to claim his cock. My tongue teased over the sensitive head, swirling over a drop of salty precum.

"Alessa," Dante moaned. His hands slid up, grasping my bared ass cheeks, then back down my thighs again.

I bobbed my head to a feverish rhythm, faltering only when his fingers played across my slit. My new husband remained at my mercy, writhing on pricey hotel sheets.

I craved too many things at once, and had too many fantasies to fulfill in one night.

Now or never, I thought, before I thrust forward and engulfed his entire cock. Dante jerked and swore, caught completely by surprise. I loved it and the power I held over him. I savored every second of having him beneath my spell.

I didn't stop until my nose pressed snugly against his balls. He trembled and quivered beneath me, his tight muscles pulled to maximum tension.

His slick fingers left my tight channel, replaced by the heat of his mouth and the playful plunge of his tongue. We took turns driving one another mad. One moment, his tongue would slide down my folds, claiming me with harsh strokes, and then I'd take him into my mouth again until his dick glided to full penetration. We both shuddered, pushed to our limits.

Dante stiffened beneath me. His hips bucked and he orgasmed on my backstroke, releasing into my mouth. The salty-sweet rush pooled over my tongue as I reduced him to guttural groans and unintelligible syllables.

At the end, he slumped his head to the pillow and gave a content sigh. I still trembled with my own need, sliding my mouth off of his dick with a wet pop.

"You're so good at that," Dante muttered from between my legs. I kissed his softening cock and stroked his balls.

"I've been wanting to try that for a while, actually."

A single roll of his body swapped our positions.

"I need to feel you inside me, and I need it *now*," I groaned out.

"And I want to taste you," he growled before tracing my wet divide with his tongue. Just as I'd held him at my mercy, Dante had me at his; I became his willing victim, writhing and arching on the bed. My hips rose and I grinded against his mouth, out of control with lust. He licked everywhere but the tiny pearl that would free me from my feverish discomfort, neglecting it.

"Dante? I can't... I need... *please!*"

His lips sealed around my clit, he sucked, and I melted. My core clenched with need, desperately wet and needing to be penetrated by more than his tongue. I whined softly as he swiped it from side to side.

"I'm close, so close," I gasped out. "I wanna come with you inside me."

Agile and fast, Dante twisted and repositioned himself, his stiffening cock a teasing presence between my thighs.

"No, I want to ride you, baby." My entire body burned for him with unmistakable yearning surpassed only by the craving to be in control. My nipples tightened to the point of pain, hypersensitive beneath the lace.

The comforter and sheets wrinkled beneath us as we rolled again. Rising above him gave me a sense of power and confidence. The way Dante's eyes roved over every inch of me made me feel sexy. Cherished. Loved.

My breaths came hard and fast, my thighs tightening and clenching to move up and down on his length. Sweat beaded upon my brow as the winding pressure built within my core.

He scraped his teeth over one pebbled nipple, teasing through the thin lace cup. A second later, he discovered the stretchy material pulled away from my tits. He tugged at the straps and freed both to the open air and the sweet torture of his lips. It was one stimulation too many, and he sent me careening over the edge.

"I love you!"

I wailed as I came, the intensity of my orgasm sweeping me along on a white-hot torrent of pleasure. A wave of ecstasy crashed over me, and as I went rigid, Dante took over, pounding my body with hard jackhammering thrusts. My breasts bounced wildly to his frenetic pace.

On his next stroke, I spasmed around his cock and he came undone, losing himself to join me in mutual orgasm. We rocked together and grinded until the last rhythmic pulse, and then finally we lay still.

"Mmm…" I sprawled across his chest, sweaty skin against sweaty skin. "That was an amazing idea."

"Agreed," Dante mumbled. "I like this black thing. Promise me you'll get more."

"I'll buy a closet of them." I giggled and kissed his cheek. "Obviously all of our baby-making was only practice."

"Definitely better now," he agreed.

"And we have a few days here to hone our skills."

Chapter 11

~ALESSA~

I returned to work Monday, refreshed and eager to see my friends. A pile of cards waited in my mailbox to congratulate me on the event.

"Do you think Castlebury is going to show up?" Julia asked during lunch.

"I don't know. He has to realize he was busted for stealing my... ah, research. Teo sent him a scathing email last week. I know that much." I popped a sweet and salty plantain chip into my mouth then gazed at the office clock.

"Crazy snooper. I always knew he was a leech." Julia tossed her yogurt cup in the trash. "Anyway, I gotta get back to work. I'm leading the afternoon tour and Pam gets to feed the fish."

"Everyone loves a feeding frenzy," I said, laughing.

My office door slammed open, the knob banging against the wall. Julia and I both jumped in our seats.

"Where the hell did you take those photographs?" Castlebury demanded.

I jerked upright in my chair and raised my eyes to the doorway. My thieving boss stood framed in front of my office, red-faced and absolutely furious. His breaths came in uneven huffs, and his hair was mussed, as if he'd come running quickly all the way from the island's dock. His wild and crazy eyes made him look like a maniac.

"Excuse me?" Julia asked.

"Get out, Ms. Sanchez," Castlebury said.

"I don't—"

"Get the fuck out," he hissed.

Julia's eyes flared wide then she rose from her chair and abruptly strode from the room.

"What the hell do you think you're doing kicking people out of my office?"

He ignored me, which was nothing new at all. "Where did you take the water horse photographs?"

"I don't know what pictures you're talking about."

"The pictures on your bloody camera," he spat.

"Are you saying, Doctor Castlebury, that you went through my personal property and downloaded files from my computer without permission?" I crossed my arms over my chest, refusing to break under his scrutiny.

His mouth gaped like a fish. I had him there, and he knew it. If he admitted to stealing files from me, he'd get fired on the spot.

"Clear out your office. I have no need for an irresponsible employee."

"I've caught you red-handed and your solution is to fire me?" I demanded. Heat flooded to my cheeks, worsening with my increasing anger. I could barely breathe, my chest so tight and constrictive that my vision swam and the room spun.

"Had I known of your laziness, I would have promoted one of your little friends instead. I was under the impression you no longer desired a position as my assistant. When was the last time you completed a full day's work in this department? Inferior quality of work and half-completed tasks, while the rest of staff and I pull your weight as well as our own. If anything, you've proven your position is entirely obsolete and you are no longer needed."

Inferior work? I stiffened. "I've had other things to do! Teo assigned me—"

"Excuses. Unless I'm mistaken, I am the department manager of the aquatics division and retain full authority of my employees." Castlebury sneered. "Go play mermaid."

Pushing to my feet, I glared at him, fury churning my stomach. "Listen, I do damned good work, and even though I've been reassigned for the summer I have been helping out and pulling my weight around here. You have absolutely no right to barge into my office and demean me like this."

"This is *my* department and I'll go wherever I damn well please. Now tell me where you found the animals. Do you not understand the value of these creatures?"

"Look, those pictures were taken by Marcy Arcillanegro at her friend's Hollywood movie studio. We mixed up cameras the last time we hung out. You can call our boss' *wife* and confirm it."

Castlebury's eyes darkened. "You and I both know the truth. You saw the beasts as well as I did." He leaned forward with his hands on my desk, staring into my eyes. "I saw two of them twenty-five years ago with my own eyes. You saw them, too, you silly little bint, and I don't know why you're hiding it, but the truth will emerge."

"You're talking crazy."

"There's money to be made in this discovery and nothing to be gained by concealing it. Think of your child."

Is he seriously trying to bribe me now? "Get out of my office."

The doctor clenched his jaw and straightened. "Very well then. I can guarantee your name becomes mud in the marine community. You'll never work anywhere beyond this little rock, and you'll never amount to anything more than a pair of large tits in a fish suit—"

"Is there a problem here?" Teo moved through the doorway, impressive and sexy as always in his beach whites. Julia hovered outside the doorway behind him. "Alessa, are you all right?"

Words failed me. All I could do was stand behind my desk, quaking with anger and indignation. I shook my head.

"We were discussing her work ethics, Mr. Arcillanegro. Nothing to concern yourself with, I assure you."

"I decide what is worth my consideration, Doctor Castlebury, and I believe *your* services are no longer required on my island," Teo informed the stunned man. "I expect your office cleared before the end of the day."

"You can't do this!" Castlebury exploded, his cheeks mottled red.

"I can do whatever I wish. You were threatening an employee and making sexually harassing remarks, both situations which I do not tolerate among my staff."

"This is a damned conspiracy!" the disgraced scientist roared. "Are you aware of what she hid? This girl concealed photographic evidence of an entirely new species."

Teo, looking unimpressed, crossed his arms over his chest. "Then you are admitting to theft as well?"

"The photos were left in plain sight!"

"In my closed office," I grunted.

"I think that the matter is clear. My wife took those photographs while we visited a dear friend in Hollywood. Are you unable to differentiate a live animal from movie magic? You are to leave by the end of the day, Doctor Castlebury, or I'll have security assist in your removal."

"You will be hearing from my lawyer about this matter. It isn't over. It isn't over by a long shot. You are both covering up the existence of creatures the world deserves to see. And I *will* find them."

The doctor stormed from the room and slammed the door behind him.

"Congratulations, Alessa."

I blinked and swung around to face Teo. "For what?"

"Your promotion." He winked at me and left as quietly as he'd entered.

***

A summer storm swept from the east to unleash sheets of refreshing rain over the island. I hadn't quite made it to the stone pathway outside of my house before the skies opened to spill a merciless torrent.

"Shit!" The water was cool against my skin, the perfect temperature for soaking in the weather — but I had my assigned work laptop in my bag and an assload of paperwork. I sprinted up the steps and reached the door as Dante opened it to usher me inside.

"Whoa, you're in early."

"I could say the same of you," Dante replied. He took my bags and shut the door behind me.

"I don't teach today and I helped Abuelo close his shop once the weather forecast reached us."

"I would have come in earlier, but we had massive drama at the aquatics center."

I told Dante all about it while I changed clothes, starting with Castlebury barging into the office to interrogate me. Apparently, Teo had been passing by on foot to the visitors center when Julia flagged him down.

"He was in the right place at the right time."

"Yeah. I'm glad Julia had the wits to get him. God, I was so pissed at first I couldn't even think." I leaned into him and giggled. "You should have seen Castlebury's face when Teo told him to pack up and leave."

Dante snorted. "Did Mr. Fancypants cry?"

"No, but he mottled up like a koi fish. Big red splotches all over his face."

Together we snickered and I further described my former manager's bugged eyes and temper tantrum as he packed his office. Everyone had watched the spectacle then we cheered at the end when he vacated the premises.

"So what happened with the photos?" Dante asked.

"According to Teo, the scientific community immediately dismissed them as clever Photoshop fakes. Then his friend Saul—"

"You mean the other dragon who visits?"

"Yeah. Him. He owns a big movie studio, so I guess he had his special effects team put together an animatronic water horse in, like, three days. Marcy said he actually plans to use it now in a film."

Dante chuckled. "It won't be the first movie to feature one of my kind, but I wager it will be the best."

"We can make a movie night out of it."

Dante's warm arms hugged me tighter. "Yes, we will. I told you all would be well."

"I know. Still, I'll be more careful in the future."

"On the subject of all being well…" He inhaled a large breath. "My father and I came to a decision today. When the herd leaves, I won't be joining them."

"What?" I twisted in his hold and studied his face.

"He granted me his blessing to remain here. My place is here with *you* and our growing child. What sort of provider would I be if I left you alone?"

"But won't you get sick?" I asked, alarmed.

"I can make it." The stubborn set of his chin dissuaded me from arguing. To be honest, I didn't want to. A small, selfish part of me had been terrified by the thought of going through the birth without him.

I barely had a tummy when the day came for his herd to travel east. I'd spent every day watching Dante for signs of regret or a change of heart, but he invited me along to say goodbye.

Helena and the three stallions came ashore to visit me one last time, the moment passing with tears and cool touches of their velvety muzzles against my cheek. I hugged my new friend tight with both arms around her neck then met a shy, golden-furred foal.

Would my baby be so tiny and delicate? I crouched to meet Zeno and Helena's baby as the young hippocampus boldly approached me on spindly, coltish forelegs.

Eventually, they retreated to the water while I remained on the shore. Dante swam out to make his personal farewells and returned after the hippocampi disappeared beneath the water.

"You're sure about this?" I asked when he was back beside me.

Dante placed his palm over my belly, igniting a surge of butterfly flutters. Tears glistened in my eyes as I realized the tiny movements had been more than my nerves. "I have never been so sure of anything in my life. My place is with you. My family."

Chapter 12

FEBRUARY

~DANTE~

Peaceful months passed from autumn into a quiet winter on the island. Teo closed the resort to tourists, seasonal workers packed their bags, and my herd — my family — left me in the care of the woman I loved. I watched Alessa grow with our child, beginning with a small baby bump to a rounder tummy.

I hid my weakening from Alessa by spending more time than usual in the water to rejuvenate myself. It helped, but nothing could replace the vast ocean and the deep currents.

The kelp forest must be beautiful now, I thought. I made do by capturing prey near the islands, but I missed the fields of kelp in the sea off the Mediterranean coasts. I missed grazing as my kind were intended to, and without the support of my people I would eventually wither until nothing remained but a shell.

It didn't help that Teo reported one of his security boats sighted Castlebury near my herd's tropical feeding zone. Because he hadn't broken any laws yet, the dragon's hands were tied.

"Dante?"

I blinked away from the television to my wife. Rubbing my drowsy eyes, I regained my senses to shoot her a warm smile. "Hm?"

"Do…?" Alessa swallowed and toyed with the edge of her blouse while studying the belly blocking her view of the floor.

"Do what?"

"Nothing," she said too quickly. "I'll make dinner."

I stood up from the sofa. "I told you I would do it. It's only fair since you did clean the entire house while I slept."

The fragile smile diminished and slipped from Alessa's face. "It's okay. You look distracted. I don't want to bother you." She scurried away and into the bathroom where she remained until I rapped on the door with my knuckles. My hearing, my strong, inhuman hearing, picked out the sound of sniffling before she muffled it with running water.

"Are you crying?"

"No!"

"Please open the door."

The door cracked open and Alessa peeked out. Despite her denial, damp tracks marked her cheeks.

"Do you regret being with me? You're distant. You never talk to me anymore."

"Is that what you've come to think, Alessa?"

She nibbled her lower lip and didn't resist when I pushed the door open further. Gently, afraid I'd broken something between us, I took her by the hands and drew her into my arms as much as her round belly would allow.

"I don't regret a single thing about what we've done or the child we've made, Alessa. I don't regret one step of the path we took or a second of our time together. You are the most valuable possession I have. I cherish you."

"What's happening to us? You barely speak with me."

Memories of my first year on land returned to me. Memories of lying in a sick bed between visits to the doctor. Abuelo took me to clinics and faith healers, hoping anyone could alleviate my suffering. By the time the humans realized what I was, I was almost dead.

I still recalled the warmth of Teo's hand as we stood at the edge of the beach, the memory of my reunion with Dad branded into my memory.

"The choice to remain behind has been harder than I expected. That, and I worry our child will one day face my challenges," I confessed. "This has nothing to do with you or regret."

Alessa gazed into my eyes and studied my face for the truth. The examination ended with a kiss and sigh of relief. "We'll find him a human woman of his own, obviously. I'll tell Julia and Pam they're only allowed to adopt a little girl if they change their mind about getting a donor.

We'll bring back arranged marriages and make it seem fashionable."

I chuckled, roused from my black thoughts.

"I mean it," Alessa continued. "What if we consider making a hippocampus dating service? There can't be a shortage of human women eager to have a man who looks like a swimsuit model."

"Lycus is rather intrigued by the idea."

"Hey, it worked for us."

"So it did," I replied, kissing her again.

"How does the rest of your herd feel about us and mingling with wicked humans?"

"There are mixed opinions. Since Father gave his approval, the remaining opponents against crossbreeding don't have a strong argument."

"Hey, it's their loss," Alessa said in my defense. "So what about your dad's, um, mate? I saw her watching me from the head of the pack beside him."

"My… you would call her my stepmother, suggested for me to bring you jellyfish."

Alessa scrunched up her nose and shook her head. "Bleh. I guess it's the thought that counts. And now I'm hungry."

"I'll get dinner going, or would you rather go pick something up?" I asked, halfway to the kitchen.

"I dunno. There's salmon in the fridge, I was going to sear that." Alessa cleared off the table. Then she scrubbed it and moved on to the kitchen counters a moment later with an expression of immense focus on her face. The salmon and our dinner had been forgotten that quickly.

"What are you doing?" I asked gently.

"Cleaning."

My brows rose. "It's already wiped down, remember? You made me take those smelly wipes to it this morning."

"Huh. Okay, I guess so. Just let me get this spot over here."

"Alessa," I moved over and tugged the sponge from her hand. "What are you doing this for?"

"My back hurts, so I want this all tidy before I lie down for the night."

"Then lie down and let me do it. I'll bring you dinner in bed."

"I don't know… You're right," she admitted. "I'll lie down. You do whatever you want."

Alessa winced and bent forward, both hands beneath her belly. Discomfort rippled across her face.

"What is it? What's wrong?" I moved to her side in an instant.

"It's only a contraction," she assured me. "I'll go sit on the sofa with my feet up until it stops."

I stared at her, surprised by her cavalier attitude. "Are you sure? I can call the doctor—"

"No, no, no. It's fine. We talked about this, remember? They're only false contractions and we'll waste the doctor's time."

Five hours later, it was after midnight and Alessa was miserable. I ran her a bath, and rubbed her back as she soaked, but nothing alleviated her discomfort.

One phone call to Marcy and Teo confirmed my theory — our baby was on the way.

~ALESSA~

My doctor and I arrived simultaneously in puffs of jasmine-scented smoke and mystery. I didn't care to question it since the nifty teleportation occurred while I was held captive by a particularly nasty contraction.

"It's a pleasure to see you again, Alessa and Dante," she greeted us kindly.

"I thought you told me the baby wouldn't be due until almost April," I panted out. My unborn child pressed one of its extremities into my ribs, introducing me to a sharp stab of discomfort. "Is my baby going to be okay? Is it too early?"

"By my previous estimation, I did believe you would deliver a few weeks from now, but this isn't a typical human birth," Dr. Thompson explained.

Marcy nodded in agreement. "I carried for eleven months, Alessa, and Javier is healthy as you can see."

"Don't worry. As I said before, you'll be my third supernatural birth, but I have years of experience delivering human babies."

I nodded and held tightly to Dante's hand, caught in the grip of a contraction, thus unable to speak to the woman. She waited patiently until the tension faded from my face.

"How far apart are the contractions?"

"One minute now," Dante answered.

My doctor confirmed my labor and readiness to birth, then Marcy helped me from my constrictive, itchy clothing. I was without a shred of modesty and quickly shed them on the open veranda. Teo could have marched a thousand dragons onto the serene space and I wouldn't have given a flying *fuck*. Nothing mattered but acquiring a modicum of comfort.

The birthing pool awaited me at the edge of the deck near a tranquil, bubbling fountain, surrounded by green ferns and a few early blooming flowers. I heard the rhythmic sound of the ocean waves crashing against the sand a few yards away. The dawn sky was awash with pale streaks of pink and lavender.

I sank into the buoyant salt water filling the pool and closed my eyes. I opened them to find Dante standing beside it, looking helpless and at a loss.

"How do you feel?"

I spared him my honest answer. "Ready," I answered. "Are you going to stay the entire ti—IME?" My voice cracked and rose sharply with pain.

"I'm not going to leave you." Dante knelt beside the birthing pool with his elbows resting over the lip. "Unless you want me to go, I'll stay right here with you. The whole way."

"No, don't go," I gasped out when the contraction ended. Marcy was right; the pain had amplified once my water broke, but the warmth of the water eased my suffering to a tolerable level. I took my husband by his shoulders and clutched him, burying my fingers into the brawny muscle.

"Then I won't go."

"You look sick," I whispered. The unbearable tension eased, allowing my fingers to loosen from his shoulders. I touched his lank hair and smoothed it back from his face. For the first time, I noticed the dark shadows beneath his eyes.

"Insignificant compared to the birth of our baby."

He was so strong. I loved this man and nothing in the world could make me regret the decision to have his child. Our child.

"What happens next?" I asked the doctor.

"For you supernaturals, I like to take a hands-off approach without interference. I'll be here if there's distress or a problem, but for the most part, you ladies seem to have instinct telling you what to do."

"Okay." *Distress*. The doctor's words echoed in my mind, a terrifying notion.

"Do I do anything?" Dante asked. "What can I do to help?"

"Exactly what you're doing now for her," Marcy said. She touched his shoulder with one hand and brushed a few strands of hair from my face with the other. "Just rub her back and stay with her. I'm gonna go talk to Teo and let him know all is well."

"Okay," I gasped on the next contraction. I was stuck on repeat, a broken record too overwhelmed by the events taking place to create intelligent discussion. To my surprise, the misery never worsened, allowing me to find enjoyment in the natural surroundings.

The next hour happened in a haze. My agony ended abruptly, flooding me with intense relief. I reached beneath me to gather the newborn, only to find my tiny gift was already floating upward to greet me.

A girl. I had a little girl. She cried a strong, healthy wail when she reached the surface, and with Dante's help I gathered our baby close to my bare breasts. Tears streamed down my face as I peeked down at tiny wisps of dark red hair and murky, cloudy gray eyes. Would they become blue eventually like Dante's or stormy gray like mine?

"You did great," Marcy said in a quiet voice, giving us some space. She and the doctor allowed us a few private moments to bond with our daughter.

After the doctor wrapped my baby girl in a fluffy white towel, she moved to the table nearby. Dante helped me from the bathing pool and into a thick terrycloth robe, my legs trembling and shaky. Marcy tucked me into a prepared guest bedroom while Dante carried our pink, surprisingly docile and calm baby back to me.

"I thought babies were supposed to scream," I whispered.

"The doctor said she had an easy transition and is perfectly healthy." Dante sat beside me on the bed and lowered our newborn into my hold.

"Do you think Phoebe fits?" I asked him. With her returned to my arms, a mellow cloud fell over me.

"It is a beautiful name," Dante assured me. He leaned close to kiss my forehead, and with one hand, he wiped the single tear sliding down my cheek.

"Will you call my mom for me?"

Dante got ahold of my cell phone and made the call to my mother. She panicked at first, and after Dante assured her that we were fine, swore she'd be on the next plane.

"She's so alert. Look at her. She's watching me."

"She's breathtaking," Dante told me.

I thought Dante would leave while Marcy guided me through nursing for the first time, but he hung by my bedside, intrigued. Marcy snapped a few candid photographs for my album then stepped out with promises to see us soon for more pictures.

We didn't remain in Teo's home for long. According to the doctor, I'd had the easiest, most stress-free birth of her career and I was free to continue my recovery at my own house. She'd check up on me later, and a nurse would arrive once or twice over the coming days to make sure I needed no assistance.

Friends and family offered all kinds of help, but in the end, the only thing I truly wanted was Dante and our little girl.

Chapter 13

~ALESSA~

Spring arrived in the blink of an eye, and with it came the return of Dante's herd. They didn't arrive a moment too soon — he couldn't conceal his exhaustion anymore, and the ocean had ceased to help him. He spent days in the bed, listless and without an appetite, awakening only to chat with me or hold Phoebe close during her nap times.

I tried to convince him to let one of the other paranormal creatures return him to his people, but he refused.

"They'll be here soon. I need to wait for them."

And he was right. One sunny, spring afternoon just after he'd begun to come around again, Dante exhibited an unusual burst of energy, dragged himself from our bed and disappeared into the water for a swim. Unable to sleep, I stayed up late nursing Phoebe and worrying over him. Evening came and went, but my mate didn't return that night or the next. Teo sent Kekoa to patrol the water for signs of him, but there were none.

Three days passed before someone laid on my door buzzer. I'd never met the man in person before, but Dante had described his father's human guise in detail. It also helped he wore Dante's swim trunks, the pair he kept hidden in Abuelo's boat by the docks in case of emergency.

"Where's Dante?"

The soaking wet man frowned at my abrupt greeting. "My son wanted to return to you, but he lacks the strength. I came in his stead." His father had a thick, almost unrecognizable accent, but I recognized hints of Dante in the way he spoke.

"Is he going to be okay?"

"In time. He needs time under the water."

Instantaneous relief surged over me, a wave so intense my knees almost buckled. I caught myself with one hand on the door frame and let out a ragged sob. Strong hands supported me beneath my elbows, surprising me as much as my uncontrollable tears.

"He loves you very much, Alessa. Enough to fight our request for him to recover."

I tried to nod, hating the terrible sounds coming from me. "I thought... when he didn't return." Another breath shuddered in and out of my lungs, then I wiped my eyes quickly with the back of my hand. "I'm sorry. Come inside. I mean, would you *like* to come inside?"

"May I see my grandchild?" he countered.

"She's sleeping, but yes, of course." I gestured for him to enter and didn't balk at the trail of water he made, accustomed to cleaning up after my husband whenever he returned from the water.

Adon followed me to the nursery where Phoebe slept, blissfully unaware of her father's absence. Bright copper-red curls covered her head.

My father-in-law leaned against the crib railing and gazed down at her through peaceful, blue eyes shared by my daughter and husband. "She is precious. I see you and my son both in her features."

"She's going to have his eyes, I think. Your eyes, I guess. They get bluer with every passing day."

A smile touched his lips. Adon stepped away from the crib and left the room, so I followed behind him curiously. "I will leave you without further interruption to your day, but I promise Dante will come back to you soon, well and whole."

"Please tell him I love him."

He nodded his head in understanding. "I will pass him your words."

Instead of opening the door to let him out, I stepped forward and threw my arms around the shifter in a tight hug. "Thank you."

Adon hesitated. His entire body became rigid in my hold, but I sensed it was from shock, rather than revulsion. "For what?"

"For giving us this chance. Thank you for listening to your son."

Seconds later, his strong arms surrounded me. I soaked in the warmth of a father's love for the first time in over a year since my dad's death. We stood together for countless seconds, maybe even minutes, my cheek against his still-damp shoulder.

"I loved his mother. Her black tail and coat never represented misfortune to me. In my eyes she was special. Beautiful. The moment I laid eyes on her I knew she was destined to be mine." Adon released me and held me at arm's length to look at me. "Much like you and Dante. When mates are fated, the bond is twice blessed, but when one is lost to early death…"

"He told me what he remembered about his mother," I ventured.

"I only know a human murdered her. A human took my beloved from me and stole Dante's mother. When he came of age and showed interest in returning to this world, I handled it poorly." Adon sighed. "I can never regain the lost years, but I can make it right between us now. Perhaps I should be the one to thank you, Alessa. You brought us together again."

After a few minutes of talking, Adon excused himself and prepared to leave.

"Adon?"

"Yes?" He paused at the door and looked back.

"There's a man out there who claims he saw a hippocampus twenty-five years ago. He… he's looking for you guys now, and he's a bad man. A really bad man." I frowned. I had a terrible suspicion about the identity of the diver who had killed Dante's mother. Was it safe to share it with them?

"Teo warned us. We are keeping close to his island."

Dante showed up at the door five days later with unshelled scallops and a bouquet of flowers. He barely dropped his gifts in time to catch me; I'd leapt into his arms and peppered his face with kisses.

"You look so much better," I admired between our soft kisses. "I was so worried."

"Forgive me, Alessa."

"Already done. I'm just glad you're all right again."

Sometime after I tired of kissing my man, I collected my net of scallops and placed my bruised bouquet in water. Dante wandered in with Phoebe in his arms.

"She has grown so much in a week," he marveled. Phoebe squirmed in his hold, gave him a gummy smile, then promptly filled her diaper.

"Here, I'll go change her," I offered while giggling at Dante's bewildered expression. "In fact, I'll get her into the bath while I'm at it."

"Okay. I'll start shucking the scallops."

"Silly girl," I cooed. I cleaned her while the tub filled.

"Dad told me you guys had a long talk!" Dante called from the kitchen.

"We did. I'll tell you everything about it when I'm out."

Soothing water surrounded my ankles once I stripped and stepped in the foaming bath. I cuddled Phoebe close and squatted to dip one wrist into the water. Perfect. We both lowered into the warm suds, and I settled her against me.

"Isn't this nice, Phoebe?"

My red-haired baby splashed and flailed, kicking up water against the cream-colored tiles and over the edge of the tub. I tried to hold on to her without success as she became a slippery mass of wriggling limbs. And tail. Seal fur and sleek scales. She dove away from me toward my toes and I screamed.

"Dante! Come here!"

My shrieks called Dante to us. His footsteps thundered through my living room floor and he burst into the open doorway, his eyes wild with worry.

"What's wrong? What happened?"

When he saw her, his features transformed from terror to astonishment. Wonder filled his handsome features as he stepped forward to kneel beside the tub. We watched together as Phoebe barrel rolled in the water and tested out her flipper like front legs. Her little tail splashed.

Thank God I used the sensitive bubble bath, and not much of it, I thought, suddenly worrying for my baby's scales. Her scales. My baby had scales. All along, we knew there was the likelihood of her changing at some point and taking her non-human body, but I'd thought she would be older.

She'd gone from a helpless infant, completely dependent on me, to an energetic and eager water foal. I cried. Tears of happiness and sorrow, an odd contrasting mix of my welling emotions, fell down my face while I watched her explore the water and eventually return to me. Big, blue eyes gazed into my face with recognition and love.

"She's radiant," Dante murmured. He'd been so silent beside us I almost forgot he was there.

His observation drew attention to her tail. Golden scales faded to fiery-red streaked with purple at the end of the fan like a magnificent sunrise. A tiny tuft of red mane decorated her graceful neck before and behind her sparkling dorsal fin.

"She's much smaller than the foals born in the water, but I think she'll be ready for the ocean soon. Maybe ready in time for our departure this year."

And with his words, my heart broke. I was no more ready to let her go than I was to see my new husband leave.

Chapter 14

~DANTE~

Phoebe took to the water as if she'd lived in it since birth. Her natural instincts kicked in, but I had to convince Alessa to allow a practice trip to Teo's island without the boat.

Her solution was to snorkel beside us, and together we frolicked under the waves while chasing colorful fish. Phoebe delighted in all manner of play favored by our youngest foals, but she especially loved our cuddles and the kisses we gave her along the way. The amazing transition between cooing infant to semi-independent foal amazed both of us.

Her thoughts came as childish babble to me, incoherent syllables that would one day form the basic components of our native language. I talked back to her as was common among our kind, while Alessa swam on oblivious to our chatter. I watched both of them as my heart welled with pride.

It took us a little less than a half hour to reach the shallow waters bordering Teo's Island. Alessa scooped up our wriggling foal, and as I emerged, I caught sight of Marcy and Teo picnicking on the beach with their son. The trio greeted us with enthusiastic waves.

"Oh my God. But she's so young!" Marcy exclaimed. "How did this happen?"

Alessa explained while I sprawled across the shore and allowed Teo's son to crawl onto my back. I'd been giving him rides since he was old enough to clutch my mane. Remaining in my hippocampus form, I chuckled and pulled my large body across the gritty sand.

Phoebe squirmed until Alessa released her to join me. She watched at first but appeared eager to emulate my actions. She tried to keep pace on her slender forelegs and delicate flippers while the tropical sun warmed our wet bodies.

"I wonder if her ability to change coincides with the herd's return," Marcy murmured.

Teo stroked his chin. "It's possible. If we had placed Javier in a challenging situation, he may have changed at a younger age."

"But I didn't put her in a challenging situation. I only put her in the bath tub. Christ, it wasn't even salt water, Teo," Alessa said. "Now she's swimming alongside us." Suddenly, Alessa looked ill. "What if she won't become my baby again?"

"She will," Marcy assured her. "She'll always be your baby. If she's anything like Javier, or my friend's daughter, Astrid, she'll change back when she's ready to nap."

Marcy's words appeared to soothe Alessa and I was never more grateful for such good friends. When it was time for the herd to leave again, this time with Phoebe and myself, I knew my wife wouldn't be alone.

Bored with me, or maybe more interested in my daughter, Javier abandoned my back and plopped down beside Phoebe instead. His brown limbs elongated, skin becoming raven hued scales. The young dragon shook out his feathered wings then pounced forward.

"You have to be very gentle with Phoebe, Javier. She's only a baby," Marcy coached him. Because dragon half-breeds aged slower than human babies, Marcy's five-year-old didn't appear to be more than a young toddler in his human form. He and Teo had similar smells, the scent of wild earth I associated with black dragons.

The shy dragonling touched noses with Phoebe and smelled her. Equally curious, Phoebe butted her small head against his snout.

"It's a shame Astrid isn't here to play with them. We'll have to arrange a playdate," Marcy said.

Dragons, playing with my child. A few hundred years ago, we would have been food for them. The thought prompted me to take my human shape so I could grin and laugh, pleased with the idea.

"What's so funny, Dante?" Alessa asked.

"Time has changed so much, is all. I think a playdate is an excellent idea. Phoebe should know other special children like her."

We played until the kids exhausted themselves. Phoebe sought out Alessa, ready to nurse, and took her human form. She fell asleep within minutes, cradled in her mother's arms.

"Why don't you two stay here tonight?" Teo invited.

"Yes, please," Marcy added. She sat beneath a palm tree, Javier asleep in lap.

"I'd really like that, thanks." Alessa smiled and looked to me for my thoughts on the matter.

"I would as well, but while you all rest I'm going to go check in with the herd. I can't wait to tell dad about her first change. He'll want to come see her."

"I believe they are out on the reefs, Dante," Teo told him. "I saw them heading out earlier today during a swim."

True to the dragon's word, I came across my people out past the reefs. A third of the herd had ventured out to graze in the open water, searching for crabs, urchins, and luscious sea grass. My father stood out, a shining beacon of golden scales, observing the feeding mares and youngsters.

"Dante, you've come." Adon glided toward me. We rubbed our muzzles in affectionate greeting.

"Phoebe made her first change today. I thought you would like to know."

Pleasure radiated through our mental link. "Good, good. We will go see her together after everyone is fed."

The ocean above us suddenly thrived with food. Our world became saturated with delicious morsels of salmon and shelled clam, inducing a feeding frenzy unlike anything I'd ever witnessed.

I refused to give in to the feeder's instinct and held back to watch. As a rule, lactating mares and foals ate first while the rest of us circled like sharks from below, prepared to ward off any predators hoping to ascend from the ocean depths. The guard had always eaten last, but now we were dispersed throughout and protection of our most helpless herdmates was everyone's responsibility.

Wait. Why is there so much fish? Where'd it all come from?

The storm of fish continued to fill the waters from above. The shadow of the boat carried past.

"No! Wait! It's a net!"

My warning came too late. Netting sliced through the water and took most of our meal with it. And countless mares. Our foals. The ones who escaped the trap screamed in panic and went rushing into the ocean depths.

I broke surface and watched the boat continue on its course, my mind filled with the terrified screams of hippocampi women and children. The trawl net dragged them along as helpless prisoners. I dove under again as Hyrum reached me.

"Dante, what's happening?"

"Do you remember the boat we saw to the east years ago? The large fishing vessel?"

"Yes, I recall," Hyrum said.

"This is a bigger version of it. It was made to capture sharks! We won't be able to free them on our own," I said.

"What can I do?"

"Go to the dragon's island and tell Alessa we need help!"

~ALESSA~

As much as I loved the sight of Phoebe in her other form, I preferred her pink skin and silken baby curls.

Teo, ever the sweet man, excused himself to allow us girls some time to chat amongst ourselves.

"Teo, I didn't mean to intrude on your family picnic," I began, only for him to smile and shake his head.

"No. It is no trouble at all. I intended to leave sometime this afternoon to make a visit to the mainland. I plan to visit a friend over a certain matter of piracy." The corner of his mouth raised in a smirk. "And to make a bribe or several to guarantee my orders will be carried out."

With our invitation secured for chilling in the cabana on the shore, I relaxed on a reclining lounge chair and napped until Kekoa arrived with cold drinks and light snacks. As I was raising my piña colada to my lips, my ears picked up the sound of a frantic cry. A horse's cry, deep and terrified.

Fear twisted my belly into a nauseating knot, ruining my taste for the alcoholic beverage. I set it aside and rose from my seat in time to see the top of an equine head. Hyrum rushed across the stretch of beach and neighed once more with his head raised high.

"Hyrum! We're over here!" I called back. I waved with my arm in the air and moved to intercept him.

We met in the middle as he shifted to his human body. A volley of Phoenician spilled from his mouth, all of it gibberish save for a single word: "Emergency."

"What happened? Slow down," I coaxed him in his language.

He shook his head and bent over with his hands on his knees, his face was flushed and he appeared exhausted. "Human boat… nets," he panted out in English. "Boat take mares. Take children. Dante plead you hurry. Need help."

"I'll go find Teo," Marcy said, her brown eyes huge in her face

"I don't have time for you to locate Teo, Marcy. Hyrum says it's urgent! If it's poachers taking their mares, it has to be Castlebury."

Marcy groaned. "Ugh. We should have known he wouldn't give up."

"I'm going with Hyrum now. Maybe I can talk reason into Castlebury or stall until help arrives. Send Teo if you can find him quickly."

"I'll get on the phone and alert the authorities, too. Fishing of any kind around Teo's islands is prohibited."

"They could be gone by the time someone gets there." I kissed Phoebe's chubby cheek and breathed in her baby sweet scent. "I'll be back, precious. I promise I'll be back." After passing my infant to Marcy, I hurried alongside Hyrum to the sandy bank.

"Do you really think that asshole is going to listen to you?" Marcy demanded.

I shook my head. "No. But I can't stand by and do nothing either."

"We can send Kekoa—"

"This is my *family*," I cried back to her over my shoulder. "I'm going."

Kekoa shook his head. "I will go with you to give whatever help I can offer."

Hyrum took me on a blindingly fast ride beneath the surface. Underwater scenery flew past me in a blur of colors and shapes, quicker than the swim I'd taken with Dante. He didn't slow until we reached the location where the herd encountered the fishing boat. From the surface, I shaded my eyes and searched, but there was no sign of the trawler.

We both sensed it at the same time. "East!" I cried, pointing with one hand as he twisted in the water. Instinct tugged at my mind and heart, telling me where to go.

It didn't take us long to find them. Startled cries and panicked voices carried to us on the ocean wind. In the distance, I saw the ship under attack. Adon sailed through the air and landed on the deck where he swung his massive tail at one of the poachers. They looked like a well-equipped mercenary squad, all hard men with muscles and armed with harpoon guns.

He fought like a beast from hell despite his disadvantage on solid ground, crushing one man beneath his heavy bulk. As another man backed to the railing and raised his weapon, Dante heaved himself up, grasped the man by the shoulder, and dragged him to a watery death. Shouts in Spanish called for them to kill the sea monsters.

A dozen, maybe fifteen men, rushed across the deck. From the size of the ship, I estimated the crew to be at least a dozen. Adon and Dante had killed three since my arrival.

As I watched, a harpoon whistled past the gold stallion, missing by a narrow margin. He seized the attacker with his teeth and hurled the man overboard. Two other poachers bobbed in the water.

Hyrum took us beneath the surface, rushing toward the netting where his herdmates were captured. Dante was there, trying to help Lycus bite through the thick ropes. I pushed off Hyrum's back to judge my mate's progress with the durable netting. He'd never bite through it.

Why didn't I think to bring a knife? There has to be a better way.

I saw the desperation in Dante's eyes and knew I had to do more. Kicking to the surface, I circled the vessel until I found an attached ladder. The fight had ended before I heaved myself over the rail. It was a bitter stalemate without a clear winner; a damaged and hurting crew against a bleeding hippocampus backed against the rail. He couldn't survive much more, and he knew it.

Under normal circumstances, I would have blushed to find so many eyes on me. The poachers stared at my bikini clad body.

"Ah. Alessa. I should have known you'd be tangled up in all of this." Castlebury stepped out from an open hatchway and roved his eyes up and down my body.

One of the poachers asked him something in Spanish that sounded suspiciously like, "What should we do with the whore?"

"I'll handle Miss Kokinos."

"Victor, you have to let them go. You're destroying the herd."

"The herd that doesn't exist?" he asked. His eyes lit up with amusement. "That bloody git had me laughed out of the conference when I arrived to show my photos. He made a fool of me, but you knew all along the photographs weren't of a mechanical creation."

"I was protecting them. You had no right to take those from my camera, but those pictures aren't what's important right now." I pointed to Adon, fighting to free his herd. "Look at him, Victor. He's hurt. Tell them to lower their harpoons."

"This is my discovery and I'll be damned if you try and sweet talk me out of it. Even a dead one will be priceless. I'll have him stuffed."

Rage flashed through me. "This isn't about sweet talking you! They won't survive! This is genocide. Those are women and children down there in your net. Babies! I assure you that if they're taken from these waters, none of them will survive and any of the stallions you left behind are sure to die, too."

"A small price to pay in the big picture."

"Do you really think the scientific community will commend you for this when they find out you've killed every single one of them? Look at this bloodshed. Look at the human lives lost here, too."

Castlebury scoffed at me. "Nonsense. Stop the dramatics, Alessa. This is why you're a failure of a scientist. You get too attached. Too emotional. If there's one herd here, there's bound to be more in another ocean."

"They're magical. They're not just some freaky new scientific discovery. This herd is their lifeline, and when separated, they become weak! They can die! They'll never survive in captivity."

"Magic. What a load of hogwash."

"Damnit, Victor, they're intelligent creatures and you can't do this!" I glanced at the net where Dante and Hyrum failed to make progress. Terrified calls of young hippocampi and their scared mothers tore at my heart.

This cold, unfeeling bastard doesn't care about anything but himself.

"They do appear to have some intelligence to them, but perhaps this animal merely submits to greater strength while wounded." He gestured to the single harpoon lance protruding from Adon's side. My father-in-law's blue eyes were filled with pain, and blood stained his dark golden fur. Droplets of red pattered to the deck beneath him.

"Please," I begged, but the man carried on as if I'd not spoken a word.

"I speared one of these beasts years ago, but I lost it. This time the scientific community will have to believe me. A shame I didn't capture the young one then."

Oh God, he means Dante, I realized. I wasn't the only one to come to the same conclusion.

Adon knew English as well as his son. I watched as the hippocampus alpha's nostrils flared and rage washed away all traces of pain.

"Victor—" I tried to blurt out a warning, but it came too late. The next events occurred in slow motion for me.

Adon's muscles tensed like a spring coil before launching him into action. He seized the doctor by his good arm, and I heard a visceral, grisly tearing sound as the mighty stallion snapped his neck to the left and right. Victor was hurled to the boat deck during the chaos, then a spear punctured Adon's chest.

"No!"

Adon didn't stop. A paddle-shaped hoof landed on Victor's shoulder.

Another harpoon bolt released, striking the hippocampus between his scaled hindquarters and furry forebody. He continued to fight as the deck dissolved once again into all-out war. I retreated from the chaos and hurried up the narrow steps leading to the bridge.

Desperate, I grabbed the fire extinguisher mounted by the hatchway and charged into the room. By the time the man inside realized my intentions, it was too late. I swung the red cylinder at his head and experienced a satisfied rush when he slumped to the deck.

"What do I do, what do I do?"

An array of buttons, levers, and blinking lights filled the control board. I searched until I found the emergency release lever for the nets then activated it without wasting any time. Through the viewport, I watched as the rising net released from the boom and splashed back into the ocean.

It was up to Dante, Hyrum, and Lycus now.

I came down again in time to hear an inhuman noise, a feral scream more terrifying than any sound a horse-like creature should be capable of making. I shivered.

My eyes drew toward the source in time to watch Adon rear up, his mighty ribs smeared with blood. He came down on one of his assailants and took another harpoon bolt. The proud hippocampus slumped to the cold deck.

"Stop! Can't you see you're killing him!"

Of course they could see, but they didn't seem to care. Castlebury was unmoving on the deck, still and bleeding — I hoped he was dead, I hoped there was nothing left in him, because if he lived, I might kill him myself.

As I searched for a weapon, Dante and Hyrum sailed over the side. The two massive stallions struck the deck, and within seconds they had thrashed, kicked, slammed, and trampled the poaching bastards mercilessly until we received cries of surrender from two remaining crewmen. Screams from the humans floating in the water, and a frantic scramble to climb aboard, announced Kekoa's arrival.

They hadn't expected sea animals to put up such a huge fight, nor had they anticipated meeting a tiger shark.

I hurried to Adon's side and knelt beside him in the blood-stained puddle. My fingers smoothed over his golden pelt while he took labored, agonized breaths.

"I'm here. I'm here, and I'm not leaving," I whispered. Leaning over him, I set my brow to his and sobbed.

"Father!" Dante appeared beside us, his expression broken. "Father, no. Please. You cannot leave us. Not now."

"Dante, I'm so sorry," I whispered. "I tried." He'd never meet his granddaughter in her hippocampus form. Never see her gracefully shooting across the waves beside her father. I was as angry as I was heartsore for my mate, unable to stop the tears flowing down my cheeks.

"He says he isn't afraid. He looks forward to reuniting with my mother."

In the next breath, he was gone.

Chapter 15

SEPTEMBER

~ALESSA~

"It's over," Marcy told me over the phone. "Teo made so many bribes the British consulate has forgotten Victor Castlebury even exists. He'll spend the rest of his life in a Mexican prison. He won't be alone, though. Most of the crew perished but the ones who survived were wanted in a few countries for similar crimes. They won't be talking about what they saw either."

"It's more than that murderer deserves," I grumbled. "More than any of them deserve. Adon may have been the only person lost, but the entire herd has been affected."

"Have they come to a decision yet?" Marcy asked.

"It was a unanimous vote. They want Dante to replace his father in leading the herd."

The months following the attack had left the herd on edge, frightened and angry. They mourned Adon's loss, but none so much as Dante. His role in the rescue of the mares and children had cemented his place in their hearts as the new leader. No longer an outcast, he had made a flawless transition into the role of his father's successor.

I made every day with my husband and child count, but as the passing weeks brought the changing of the seasons, I knew the herd would move on when fall arrived. They had to.

I never wanted to see Dante suffer on land again, and I'd sooner die than allow Phoebe to experience the pain he endured to be with us. A need to keep her healthy superseded my desire to have her beside me.

I joined Dante on the beach after ending my call with Marcy. The ocean-scented wind tousled my hair as I moved up to his side.

"I can't believe it's time to go already."

"I don't want to leave," Dante confessed. "I don't want to rip Phoebe away from her mother and leave you here alone."

"I can make it alone, Dante, but *they* can't make it without you. Look. Look at me," I told him, touching his face. "There's a hundred horses out there counting on you right now. On *you*, baby. I don't want to separate from you… I don't want to watch you both swim away, but we knew this day was coming."

He kissed me hard, lips demanding and desperate against my mouth. At the end, I wrapped my arms around his shoulders and hugged him.

"I'll miss you both every day. Not one day will pass without you in my thoughts."

"And I won't go one night without you in my dreams," Dante replied.

"What if I offered another solution?" Teo's regal baritone announced behind us. I turned my face from Dante's shoulder to see the immaculate overlord of our island in his human guise crossing the beach.

"Another solution?" I asked, curious.

"What if we made a home for the hippocampus herd here? A permanent home of their own to dwell year-round, without an unnecessary migration."

"There wouldn't be enough food to sustain us, Teo. We migrate to allow the underwater flora a chance to recover, or we risk overgrazing—"

"I'm aware," Teo said. He wore a mysterious smile on his handsome face, piquing my curiosity. "But are you aware of *my* gift?"

"Gift?"

"Each of us dragons has a gift, a magical talent so to speak. I commune with animals and control the growth of plant life. Kekoa and I have recently found a trio of islands to cultivate, the distance no more than two hours by water."

"You can make a permanent home for us?" Awestruck, Dante stared at our mutual friend in disbelief. "If that's true, it'll put an end to our migration route and the risk to the herd."

"But why now?" I asked. "Why has this idea never come up before?"

"It was mentioned. Once. Adon, however, was not a trusting horse. He felt beholden to me for the time your herd stayed. Plus, I think memories kept him going back to Greece."

"My mother," Dante said in a low, thick voice.

"Indeed," Teo replied. "Of course, it will take some time for your new home to flourish, and for that, I apologize."

"One more migration." Dante's gaze returned to the water. "Thank you for this, Teo. I only need to keep them safe one more time."

"About that…" Teo's grin widened. "I have asked a favor of a dear friend from Japan. His daughter is en route as we speak to escort your herd to the Mediterranean islands. No shark or orca will dare to tangle with an Asian water dragon."

Dante's eyes bulged from his face. "A water dragon?"

"Yes. Thus eliminating the need for the rear guard. No more hippocampi will die needlessly. Your numbers have diminished enough."

I couldn't stop crying and I couldn't stop hugging Teo. I don't remember running over to him, but suddenly I was clinging to him and sobbing into his shoulder.

"Thank you!"

"How could I call myself a conservationist if I stood idly by? The hippocampi didn't naturally diminish. The blame for their suffering lies at the feet of mankind, and I have spent decades fighting this injustice with human money," the dragon said.

"When will your friend arrive?" Dante asked.

"Otohime shall arrive tomorrow, ready to travel alongside your group."

"Thank you. *Thank you*," I told him again as I kissed his cheek.

"I can't begin to tell you how much I appreciate this," Dante said, appearing to be in shock. "You'll have our gratitude, Teo. This is…" My husband inhaled a deep breath, moved beyond the ability to find words.

"Return to us in the spring and live happy, peaceful lives," Teo replied. "Such is enough thanks for me."

***

They left at dawn two days later. From the privacy of Teo's personal island, I was treated to the awe-inspiring sight of a hundred equine heads bobbing on the surface. Dante faced me in silence, while I cradled Phoebe in my arms.

"I'll think of you both every single day," I whispered.

"You will always be in our thoughts. We'll come back to you, Alessa, safe and whole. I promise."

We shared a tender farewell kiss then I hugged my daughter tight against me. Phoebe grinned and patted my cheeks with her tiny palms. She appeared too small and helpless, too young to be going out to sea, but I knew better. She was a natural in the water, her hippocampus form sleek and energetic.

"Be a brave girl for your mama," I told her as I kissed her cheeks. Dante scooped her up when I was done.

"I will take the best care of her, Alessa. I promise she'll come to no harm," Dante said. "I swear on my life."

"I know. I'll be here, waiting for you. For all of you."

Dante carried Phoebe into the water. As a human child, she hadn't mastered walking, but oh how she could swim. Tears blurred my vision as I stood vigil, watching my loved ones disappear into the ocean.

The enormous water dragon made her appearance, a majestic creature in varying shades of blue. In the blooming sunlight, her enormous eyes shined like gemstones. Her skin resembled lapis lazuli, a field of blue with a pattern of golden lines. As quickly as she broke surface, the serpentine monster disappeared beneath the sparkling waves and faded completely from view.

"She will protect them, Alessa. Have no fear of that," Teo said quietly.

"I know, it's just…" *I will not cry. I won't let their last sight of me be with tears running down my face.*

Marcy, sensing my inner turmoil, stepped up and wrapped her arm around my shoulders.

One by one, members of the herd blinked out of sight. I watched Hyrum and Lycus race one another, mimicking dolphins as their long bodies skipped like stones into the horizon. The last hippocampus to dip below the surface gleamed midnight beneath the dawn sky. He gazed at me with love in his gentle eyes, then sank into the eternal blue.

I bottled my pain inside and refused to allow a single tear to fall until my husband was out of sight and oblivious to my heartbreak. One single thought helped me steel myself against the wrenching pain.

If all went well, the herd would never have to leave again.

Epilogue

FEBRUARY

~ALESSA~

With Phoebe's first birthday approaching, I fell into the deepest, blackest depression I'd ever felt. Teo gave me time off from my work to pull my thoughts together, but nothing brought me joy.

Had they survived their journey?

Were they well?

Did my baby remember me the way I remembered her? I could have molded Phoebe's likeness into clay, every feature of her angelic face burned into my memory. Would I be a stranger to her?

Mom struggled to reach out to me, and eventually, she and my grandmother surprised me with a New Year's visit, courtesy of a meddling dragon and his wife. We had plenty of time to spend together while the resort was closed for the winter, our family bonding interrupted only by my duties to the aquatics center as the manager.

Of course they asked about Dante and Phoebe and I couldn't lie to them. Sobbing, I told them everything and shared the precious photographs I kept in a locked safe. Grandma perused my photos in silence as I babbled, and at the end, she turned her misty gray eyes up to me. "Your family is very beautiful, Alessa. They will return soon. Very soon."

"I can't believe these stories are true," Mom whispered. She raised her eyes to my grandmother. "Everything you told me as a child. All of those stories are real."

"It's all true, Mom. Dragons and genies, too. We even have a shark shifter." I embraced the truth, experiencing a strange sense of catharsis in revealing my pain to them without more excuses and lies.

"Many people in Greece claim to have mermaid blood in their families," Grandmother said as she took our hands. In hindsight, it made a strange sort of sense — her hair had never lost its ruby red hue or brilliant shine. Her features were surprisingly unmarred by wrinkles and signs of age. The three of us could pass for sisters. "But it's always been true for us. *My* mother was born from a mermaid."

I laughed and sniffled at the same time. "Dante said mermaids are frightening creatures."

"She could be very frightening," Grandma agreed with a fond smile on her face. "But she loved me very much. She would be proud of you."

Their visit pulled me back from the abyss, but after their departure my upbeat mood diminished, and the despair sank its claws into me again.

Teo explained that the soul bond was both a gift and a curse. By accepting Dante, he had gifted me a part of his soul, and in return, I'd given him part of mine. That bond was how I had found him during the attack, and our prolonged separation placed strain on the link.

Sometimes I cried at night, and no amount of reminiscing over digital videos or memories could soothe me. I told myself they were alive and well, that the feeling of warmth creeping into my heart was a sure sign Dante and our child were happy somewhere. I took up hobbies, met with friends, and eventually, like dark clouds obliterated by the return of the sun, the dismal mood drifted away.

Five days before Phoebe's birthday, I awakened truly happy for the first time in weeks. I showered, brushed my teeth, and I visited the beachfront spa for a full body treatment.

I even gifted myself cheesecake without guilt and spent the evening with Abuelo, helping him serve food to his customers.

"I'm glad to see you on your feet again, Alessa. I worried for you." He smiled at me from behind the counter.

"It feels good to be up again," I admitted to him. "I don't know why... I just felt really great today."

My sunny mood continued, lasting into the next few days. I took up jogging to burn the excess energy coursing through me, and I returned to our aquarium, as eager to hang out with Pam and Julia as I was to resume working full time.

The influx of new employees kept me busy. The summer before had been so hectic that both Pam and Julia had both helped out, but this year I really needed to choose a new assistant manager. When I couldn't decide, the girls drew straws to tease me. I remained stumped until Teo phoned me, laughing, and said to promote both. With the shadow of the doctor finally dissipated, our workplace thrived.

Ultimately, I decided to wait until his return before sharing our greatest secret with Pam and Julia. As far as our friends knew, my husband had gone home to Sicily for his father's funeral and I'd grudgingly allowed him to take Phoebe along to meet her extended family.

"We know there's more to it than that, chica," Julia had said gently. "And when you're ready to tell us, you'll tell us."

"Thanks, girls. I mean it."

I hugged the two women and stepped outside onto the residential path. The setting sun cast golden colors over the blue water, reminding me of the first night I invited Dante to my bed.

Kekoa stumbled onto my porch as I pulled my house keys from my purse. I'd never seen the shark less than graceful before. Or naked. Both realizations shocked me.

"They're back," he gasped out, winded. "I swam as quickly as I could and rushed to meet you. He's leading the herd to their new home now."

"So soon? How long before they're here?"

"Thirty minutes at the most. Perhaps an hour. The water dragon has many talents, it seems, and hasty travel is one of them."

While the five months apart had felt like years, each minute dragged for an eternity. I waited barefoot at the edge of the shoreline with my eyes on the twilit water.

Two equine heads broke the surface, one black as midnight skies, the other copper-red like autumn leaves. Like the sun I had admired during my walk home.

"She grew!" With a couple inches on her body, and at least a few pounds, a toddler hippocampus foal slid from the water with the tide. She transformed on the damp sand, running on two chubby legs toward me. I fell to my knees and swooped her into my arms.

"Mama. Maaa."

"She remembers me!" My laughter was thick with uncontrollable tears. Phoebe patted my slick cheek with her hands and gazed up at me as I hugged her tight.

"Mamaaa."

"Yes, baby. I'm your Mama. And I love you so, so much."

I turned my tearful eyes to Dante as he moved toward me on two legs. Nothing about him had changed, his every inch still wondrously sexy and all mine. "She remembers me," I repeated again, overcome with emotion.

"I told her about you every day," Dante whispered. He crouched down beside us in the sand and wrapped us both in his embrace. He was warm against me, my body remembering all of his chiseled angles as if he'd only left yesterday.

"You came home early."

"I couldn't let you miss Phoebe's first birthday. I know there will be many more together, but we both wanted to be here for this. For you."

For the first time in months, tears of joy flowed down my cheeks, contrasting the anguish that sought to drown me during their absence. My family was home in my arms where they belonged.

And thanks to Teo, we'd never be separated again.

The End

About the Author

VIENNE SAVAGE enjoys writing as an outlet for her creativity. She is a video gamer by nature and enjoys watching movies and reading novels by Stephen King, Mary Higgins Clark, Scott Lynch, Mercedes Lackey, Tolkien, and Michael Crichton among others. Vivienne currently lives in Texas with her two children.